THE BONE SHAKER

NewCon Press Novellas

Set 1: Science Fiction (Cover art by Chris Moore)
The Iron Tactician – Alastair Reynolds
At the Speed of Light – Simon Morden
The Enclave – Anne Charnock
The Memoirist – Neil Williamson

Set 2: Dark Thrillers (Cover art by Vincent Sammy)
Sherlock Holmes: Case of the Bedevilled Poet – Simon Clark
Cottingley – Alison Littlewood
The Body in the Woods – Sarah Lotz
The Wind – Jay Caselberg

Set 3: The Martian Quartet (Cover art by Jim Burns)
The Martian Job – Jaine Fenn
Sherlock Holmes: The Martian Simulacra – Eric Brown
Phosphorous: A Winterstrike Story – Liz Williams
The Greatest Story Ever Told – Una McCormack

Set 4: Strange Tales (Cover art by Ben Baldwin)
Ghost Frequencies – Gary Gibson
The Lake Boy – Adam Roberts
Matryoshka – Ricardo Pinto
The Land of Somewhere Safe – Hal Duncan

Set 5: The Alien Among Us (Cover art by Peter Hollinghurst)
Nomads – Dave Hutchinson
Morpho – Philip Palmer
The Man Who Would be Kling – Adam Roberts
Macsen Against the Jugger – Simon Morden

Set 6: Blood and Blade (Cover art by Duncan Kay)
The Bone Shaker – Edward Cox
A Hazardous Engagement – Gaie Sebold
Serpent Rose – Kari Sperring
Chivalry – Gavin Smith

THE BONE SHAKER

Edward Cox

NewCon Press
England

First published in the UK by NewCon Press
41 Wheatsheaf Road, Alconbury Weston, Cambs, PE28 4LF
June 2019

NCP 196 (limited edition hardback)
NCP 197 (softback)

10 9 8 7 6 5 4 3 2 1

ISBN:

978-1-912950-21-8 (hardback)
978-1-912950-22-5 (softback)

Cover art and internal illustration by Duncan Kay
Cover layout by Ian Whates

Minor Editorial meddling by Ian Whates
Book layout by Storm Constantine

One
Strange Company

Deep inside the Great Forest, night had cast its shroud.

The air was rife with the damp and earthy scent of leaf-mould. Thin tendrils of mist crept over twisting roots, weaving between skeletal trees like lost ghosts searching for a place to haunt. A new moon hung in a clear sky, its blue-grey light casting long shadows in the forest. It was a chill night, not long from winter's passing, and the first flowers of spring had started to bloom. Cold and colourless in moonlight, they served as a teasing promise of warmth from a summer yet to come.

Sir Vladisal of Boska stood atop a ridge, her silver armour dulled by dirt and moss. The forest floor sloped away from her, down into a moon-bathed clearing where mist hung as a thin veil a foot or so above the ground. Behind Vladisal, her women stood shoulder-to-shoulder along the ridgeline: some eighteen knights and five archers in all. Loyal and brave, their collective breaths rose in cold, spiralling plumes.

With a gauntleted hand, Vladisal pushed back dark and lank hair from her face. Her eyes trained on the small figure a little further down the slope. Statue-still, Abildan the assassin stood with her back to the knights, watching the clearing below with limitless patience that irritated Vladisal.

She looked back at her company. Each knight was as grime-smeared as their captain; each of them stripped of House colours, wearing no helm, carrying no shield. In the depths of the Great Forest, these brave knights of Boska were far from home.

Üban, the oldest among them, stepped forward. Thickset and gruff, the veteran knight was clearly in ill temper as she wiped moisture from her face.

"Damned fool!" she growled, indicating to Abildan. "What's she waiting for?"

"I am unsure," Vladisal said. "Perhaps she senses the approach of our reinforcements." Though, in truth, this statement was made more from hope than any genuine expectation.

Üban cursed under her breath. "I don't like it, Vlad. Nor do the women. These woodlands feel dead."

She was right. For four days Abildan had been leading the company through the Great Forest, and they had not heard the sound of a single living thing since breaking camp two mornings past. Vladisal could see the trepidation in the eyes of her knights. Not for the first time since leaving Boska, she questioned her own judgement. They were all beginning to understand that their guide enjoyed her little games and secrets.

"Stay with the women," she told Üban before carefully making her way down the slope to Abildan.

The stillness was unnerving, as if the forest itself held its breath. Only the occasional clank of armour broke the silence like nervous twitching in an uncomfortable moment. Aware of the sound her footfalls made upon dead leaves and needles, Vladisal came alongside Abildan and stared at her expectantly. Instead of speaking, the assassin raised a curt hand, demanding continued silence.

Vladisal bit back an angry retort. It would not do well for her knights to see her so easily ordered. She glared, gripping the pommel of her sword.

A clear head shorter than most women, Abildan's body was slender and lithe. She wore no armour, only a loose fitting shirt and hose of a dark green cloth. She wore a black leather waistcoat, which also served as a baldric for slim crossbow bolts. A short, curved sabre was sheathed upon her back; at her waist hung a small crossbow. No boots covered her bare feet. She did not seem to feel the cold as normal women - but then, the assassin was no normal woman.

Abildan had no hair as such, only a short, pale fur that covered her head and face, her hands and feet, and most likely the rest of her body. Her facial features were gaunt and angular; ears elongated to points. And her eyes that remained so focussed on the clearing below were yellow, almost luminous in the moonlight. They were the eyes of a cat.

Abildan blinked, once, slowly. "Someone is coming." She sniffed the air. "A child." Her feline face amused, she gave Vladisal a sardonic smile. "He's running for his life, but I don't think he's going to make it."

With a shiver, Vladisal studied the tree line on the opposite side of the clearing. She saw and heard nothing at first, and wondered if Abildan was mistaken. But then a low moan drifted through the forest. It came again, a little louder this time, followed by the sounds of something thrashing through the undergrowth.

The knights lining the ridge clearly heard it too. Many of them prepared to draw weapons.

"Keep your women at bay, Sir Vladisal," Abildan warned. "Their lives may depend on it."

Vladisal sliced her hand through the air. "Hold!" she ordered, and the knights obeyed.

Üban's face was pensive, and Vladisal knew what the old knight was thinking. The vague hope of reinforcements arriving had diminished to nothing, as insubstantial now as the ghostly mist that hung above the clearing floor.

The sound of thrashing grew louder, closer. A figure stumbled into the open. As Abildan had predicted, it was a child, a young boy, and in the moonlight his youthful face was creased with terror.

The boy clutched at his throat. Dark blood ran between his fingers and soaked his jerkin. He took a few more faltering steps, gave a sob, and collapsed to the clearing floor with a swirl of mist. Unconscious or dead, he lay face down, unmoving.

Vladisal prepared to rush to the boy's aid, but Abildan gripped her arm and held her back with surprising strength.

"A pointless act," she stated. "The child is already dead."

"How can you know that?" Vladisal snapped.

"Tactics." The cat-like assassin resumed scanning the tree line. "That child is a trap, sent ahead to entice you out of hiding. Perhaps, for now, it might be wiser to wait and see what he was running from, yes?"

The forest moaned.

A second figure emerged from the shadows and entered the clearing. A woman. She shuffled towards the boy, no urgency in her movements whatsoever. In the pale moonlight, her face was that of a corpse's: ashen, drawn, mottled with rot. Her hair was matted with dirt and leaves, as were her peasant's clothing. Her eyes shone with an eerie blue luminescence. She released another moan, but it was choked off as two tentacles slithered from her mouth and lashed at the air.

"By the Mother," Vladisal whispered. "What is this?"

"One of your enemy's tree-demons," Abildan said, matter-of-factly. "The dead have been merged with the forest, just as I warned you."

More tentacles burst from the woman's body, tearing through her rotten clothes, whipping blood into the cold air. They coiled around her torso, as though forming protective armour.

Merged with the forest… they were roots, not tentacles – wood that was as pliable as flesh.

Aware that her knights were sharing her repulsion, Vladisal watched as the woman made it to the boy. She dropped to her knees, clumsily, like her legs were no longer strong enough to hold her weight. The roots lengthened from her mouth, probing the boy's body. One slithered into the wound already on his neck; the other ripped away his sleeve and tore strips of wet flesh from his arm – strips of flesh that it drew back into the woman's mouth.

A monster feeding on a child.

Vladisal's stomach turned. She prepared to draw her sword.

"Act now and you will lose the advantage, Sir Knight," Abildan warned, her voice calm and icy. "Be assured that more tree-demons are coming. If we allow them to gather, to feast, then the boy becomes bait for a trap of our own."

"Are you sick?" Vladisal hissed.

Abildan continued as if the knight hadn't spoken at all. "When the time comes, it is important that we maintain the higher ground. These creatures are mindless and lumbering. They cannot move swiftly, yet they will be great in number. Better for them to come to us."

Vladisal thought she might strike the assassin's feline face. As if sensing this, Abildan turned to her with a mocking expression as though deliberately challenging her authority.

"Agree or not, without reinforcements, you know my tactics are sound." She narrowed yellow eyes. The forest came alive with movement. "Perhaps you should ready your archers."

"Archers," Vladisal said to Üban.

Evidently sickened and angry, Üban signalled the order with snappish movements. The archers stepped forth between the knights, quivers full of arrows, bows strung and ready.

"Here they come," Abildan sighed.

As the ghoulish woman continued feeding, hollow moaning accompanied the sound of movement in the forest. Small blue lights seemed to float through the trees. Eyes, Vladisal realised, the glowing eyes of tree-demons.

Morbid forms lumbered into the clearing. Twisted by corruption, fleshy roots protruding from their bodies, coiling around them, snaking from their mouths, they came on unsteady feet but with ravenous intent. One after the other, creeping from the forest, they headed straight for the dead boy. Men and women, old and young. The reek of decay and gargled moans filled the air.

"I cannot stand and watch," Vladisal said.

The first of the horde had reached the boy and were jostling with the woman for a taste of blood and meat.

And still more emerged from the trees.

"This is madness!"

"Do not be so eager, Sir Knight. You will have vengeance for the boy soon enough." Abildan unhooked the small crossbow from her belt, and drew back the string. Selecting a bolt from her baldric, she quite calmly slid it into place. "Remember - the magic that animates these monsters is like an infectious disease. When they come for you, sever their heads, do not let their mouth-roots sting you."

There had to be thirty abominations in the clearing now, with still more arriving, each hungering for the boy's blood. They fought over the corpse with slaps and punches as weak as they were mindless. Fleshy roots flailed and clashed.

Vladisal would allow this ungodliness to pass no longer.

"Hold to your sick tactics if you wish, Abildan, but that is not the Boskan way." With an angry noise, she drew her sword and turned to her women. "Bear arms!"

All along the ridge, knights drew weapons - Üban most keenly of all.

"For Boska!" Vladisal shouted, and she led the charge down the slope.

Two
Monsters

Üban's heart hammered as she followed her captain down the slope.

Sword in hand, the old knight's eagerness to cleave head from neck filled her ears with the rushing of blood. Behind her, the Knights of Boska echoed Vladisal's battle cry, and the sound of the charge drowned out bestial moaning made by the unholy merging of corpses and forest life. Yet, as she neared the fray, Üban's battle-lust became tinged with despair.

Vladisal had gone too far ahead. She stormed the cluster of tree-demons as if she could best them all singlehandedly. She hacked and slashed, sending her foes scattering in all directions. By the time Üban and the rest of the women met their enemy, a line of monsters stood between them and their captain.

"Volley!" Üban bellowed.

From up on the ridgeline, archers loosed arrows. Barbed heads hissed into the clearing, thudding into rotten limbs and wooden shells of the ghoulish horde. But the monsters paid no mind to their injuries, and they shambled headlong into the charge, seeking only the taste of blood.

"Aim for the heads!"

The next volley found more success. Three monsters collapsed to the ground, skulls punctured, roots thrashing in death throes. One, a young woman, had the shaft of a crossbow bolt protruding from her eye.

Üban felt a fresh surge of anger and frustration as she joined the fight and took the head from an elderly man's shoulders. She had not given the second order; it had come from Abildan, and Üban again wondered why Vladisal tolerated her presence. The assassin was a feliwyrd, a sorcerous

10

merging of human and mountain cat, and such creatures were not to be trusted.

A third volley downed four more monsters, but the army of tree-demons was so great in number now that it hardly made a difference. The Boskans were a band of five archers and less than twenty knights facing a horde that just kept growing.

Üban roared. Another foe fell.

The roots wrapped around the torsos of the tree-demons were strong and hard, but those that lashed from their mouths like the tongues of serpents were pulpy and rotten as their exposed flesh. Üban chopped the roots from the mouth of a monster so vile and emaciated that age or gender were impossible to tell, but two more appendages slithered from the rotten maw to replace them. With a grunt, Üban lopped the monster's head from its shoulders.

All about, the Knights of Boska slew their enemy with little resistance. Body after body fell in an endless wave of slaughter, but only a killing blow to the head could deaden their roots and hunger, and extinguish the lights in their eyes. The noise of the battlefield was not that of usual combat; only the thuds of metal on flesh and wood filled the clearing. Üban redoubled her efforts, cleaving a path towards Vladisal.

To her right, mighty Dief crushed skulls and cracked bones with her huge hammer, her teeth gritted, her strength tireless. To Üban's left, graceful Luca sliced flesh with a sabre in one hand, and split wood with a hatchet in the other.

"There must be three-score of them at least!" Luca shouted, decapitating the grim vision of an old woman. "And still more arrive!"

For every monstrosity they slew, the forest spat out a replacement.

"At this rate we'll be fighting till dawn."

"Let them come," Dief grunted, swinging her hammer. "All the more to send back to the hells."

But it wasn't that simple.

Whatever curse had merged their dead bodies with the forest, these monsters had once been simple village folk. They were innocent victims compelled from the grave by a dark magic.

Üban stepped back as Dief swung a murderous blow with her hammer. The head of a peasant man disappeared into a wet mist.

A small girl, no more than a babe, came at Üban. Her eyes luminescent, she reached out as if searching for safe arms to nestle in. She made a choking, gurgling sound. Roots thrashed in her mouth like trapped snakes fighting to be free. With a silent plea to the Mother God, Üban

11

thrust her blade into the girl's mouth, and twisted. The top of her head flipped open like a bloody hatchway, and she fell, roots coiling in her remains.

A scream split the night air.

The sheer volume of monsters prevented Üban reaching Vladisal, and she began to panic.

"Flanks!" she commanded. "Draw out the centre!" And her blade passed through yet another decayed neck. "We must fight through to Vlad," she told Dief and Luca.

"I see her," Dief replied. "She's surrounded."

"Wait," said Luca. "No!"

Üban felt a knot in her gut. At the clearing's centre, Vladisal had fallen, and the tree-demons were upon her.

"To Vladisal!"

The call blazed through the Knights of Boska like frenzied fire.

In her heart, Vladisal had known the boy was dead before she reached him. But she stood astride him nonetheless, protecting his bloodied ruins with all the rage she could muster. Anger blinded her, deafened her to the sound of knights fighting.

Just as Abildan had warned, the enemy showed no remorse and were many in number. It was as if death had twisted them into a corrupted mockery of life that acted only on some basic, ravenous instinct.

Vladisal maintained a protective circle around the boy. She stopped distinguishing child from adult, man from woman; they were monsters, one and all, and as each fell under her blade, the dulling of their luminous eyes was the only true sign that their hunger was at an end.

A grisly face, its lips gnawed away, came forward with a tentacular grin. Feeble and emaciated, one of its eyes rotted to nothing, it reached for Vladisal with long, claw-like fingers. Its mouth-roots whipped for her face. Dark blood sprayed as its head fell from its neck. Another ventured towards the knight, falling in similar fashion, as they all did.

A scream filled the air.

Shouting a curse, Vladisal felled another beast, but as she raised her sword again, she felt pulling on her leg.

It was the boy. He was alive!

Clutching at Vladisal's armour with red-slicked hands, the boy's whole body shook and convulsed. Vladisal felt a momentary surge of hope within the maelstrom. It quickly vanished as the boy's eyes glowed with blue light, and he coughed slim, snake-like roots from his mouth.

He clawed at Vladisal's leg, breaking fingers upon hard armour. Instinctively, Vladisal batted him away with a backhand. Another monster came at her. She skewered it through the gut, her blade slipping between the coils of roots wrapped around its body like armour.

It was a mistake.

The coils tightened on the sword, and Vladisal couldn't wrench it free. The monster shambled forward, sliding further down the blade. Vladisal lost her grip, stumbling backwards, and the enemy was upon her.

Roots wrapped around her arms, too many to shrug off. More probed at her armour. In panic, Vladisal kicked out, catching the nearest tree-demon high on the chest. This action scattered the monsters, but also toppled Vladisal. She fell to her back on the clearing floor.

Someone shouted her name. A volley of arrows punctured the tree-demons closest to her.

A small figure crawled up Vladisal's prone body. Eyes glowing, mouth open and roots lashing, the boy gurgled at her.

Vladisal closed her hands around his throat, holding him off. One mouth-root struck at her gauntlet while the other attempted to sting her face. Hands tugged at Vladisal's legs, banging upon her armour, as though the monsters were trying to break a crab's shell for the soft meat underneath.

Where is the mercy? Vladisal thought as she snapped the boy's neck.

The lights of his eyes did not fade. His roots continued to whip for Vladisal's face. She knew in that moment that she had failed, and the ungodly horde would have its meal.

The boy stiffened and fell limp in her grasp.

The light in his eyes finally died. He fell sideways, and Vladisal saw the crossbow bolt embedded into the back of his head. More bodies fell as a curved sabre whirled among them with arcs of moonlight.

Abildan.

In utter silence, the assassin moved with such speed and grace it was hard to tell if she was fighting or dancing. So confident in her abilities, so sure of her surroundings, she carved a murderous circle around Vladisal like a deadly wind, a subtle firestorm among crops, scattering heads wherever it burned. And then, as quickly as she had arrived, Abildan was gone, leaving carnage in her wake.

Vladisal scrambled to her feet and retrieved her sword just as Üban reached her. Dief and Luca were close behind. The entire company had cut a path through the enemy to reach their captain, but now the tree-demons surrounded them.

I should have listened to Abildan, Vladisal thought. They were vastly outnumbered.

But the monsters attacked no more.

A stiff wind picked up and blew across the clearing. It brought sweeter and earthier scents, chasing away the reek of decay. The tree-demons lost interest in their prey. They began creeping back into the forest, disappearing among the trees, as if following some silent instruction borne on the wind.

Some of the knights hacked down a few stragglers, but others made to follow the monsters and continue the battle.

"Stand down!" Vladisal snapped.

Her command was obeyed.

In a few moments, the knights were alone in the clearing. Not a sound disturbed the forest.

Astonished, the women of Boska surveyed the slaughter that lay at their feet, giving each other disbelieving looks.

Luca swore, her honest face troubled. "They out-matched us six to a woman at least. They had us beat! Why leave?

"Who can understand the reason of monsters?" Üban said. The old knight's face was unreadable as she watched the tree line.

Vladisal followed her line of sight and saw Abildan slip into the shadows of the forest.

Three
Higher Ground

Death permeated the air. The remains of tree-demons were literally smeared across the battlefield. The magic which had animated these corpses, which had merged them with plant life, had died. Supernatural putrefaction had set in, liquefying flesh and bone, rotting wood to mulch. While Luca and Dief searched for fallen comrades among the foul-smelling mounds, Üban and the knights watched the trees for any sign of a fresh attack.

Sir Vladisal stood alone, observing proceedings, her thoughts grim. Her gaze travelled up the slope to where the company had stood before the battle. Her five archers still lined the ridge, nervously guarding the clearing.

She should never have led such a reckless charge against the enemy. Was it pride that had stood in the way of taking Abildan's advice - a need to save face in front of her women?

Vladisal felt her soul darken. These were desperate times indeed.

Üban approached. The old knight carried a haunted look, and when she spoke, her voice was a low growl.

"There's nothing out there but trees. It's as if the demons simply vanished." She snorted. "And I see the feliwyrd is still missing. Perhaps she has deserted us for good this time."

Abildan had been absent since the battle's conclusion. The bitterness in Üban's voice was evident; she loathed the assassin, and not without good reason. But as contentious a presence as Abildan was, no one could deny that the Knights of Boska would be hopelessly lost in the Great

Forest without her guidance.

"I should have listened to Abildan, Üban. We should have kept the higher ground."

"What difference would it have made?" The bitterness in Üban's tone grew deeper. "The battle was still won."

"No. We were Lucky. The Bone Shaker withdrew her army. You know that, old woman."

Üban gave a resigned sigh. "Tonight, I do not feel proud to be a Knight of Boska. These were humble village-folk we slew. The Mother has cursed us."

"No. These people were damned by magic long before they reached us. There is no shame in our actions. We simply acted as we had to, and gave them peace from torment."

"Then what of Elander?" Üban retorted. "What if that poor boy has already been…" She sighed again. "I do not think Duchess Mayland would see things as simple were her son to fall foul of the Bone Shaker's magic."

Vladisal's gut twisted. The older knight's blunt manner was close to shattering an already fragile atmosphere, and a heated debate in front of the women would not help matters. Still, she had a point.

The son of their duchess was the prisoner of a madwoman called Dun-Wyrd. Elander was an infectious youth, barely twelve summers old, full of life, full of kindness. Vladisal was his champion, his protector; and she already felt as though she had failed her charge. What horrors, what tortures, did that sweet child face in the clutches of a Bone Shaker and her dark magics?

With a heavy voice, Vladisal said, "Abildan does not believe that Dun-Wyrd will add Elander to her dead army."

"Ah, the feliwyrd again." Üban hawked and spat. "Then why does she think the Bone Shaker wants him?"

Vladisal looked to the ground. "She says she does not know."

Üban sucked air over her teeth. "If we are to trust in everything Abildan says, then surely Redheart would have returned with reinforcements by now."

"Have faith, old woman. Redheart will return. She will find the Forest Dwellers and bring them to our side."

"She has been gone two days already, Vladisal."

"And you think I don't know that? We cannot change the situation as it is, Üban. We will continue our search for Elander. We will have faith that Redheart will return in time and that Abildan is not as untrustworthy as you believe."

"Aye, lass." Üban's tone lost its sharp edge. "I'll pray for that."

Luca made her way over. She looked shaken, her face pale.

"Damned tragic. Sir Theodora and Sir Brennik – both dead." She took a deep breath and looked over the clearing. "I've ordered them prepared for burial."

Vladisal nodded sadly. "A grim night, but we have survived."

"And gained a frightening insight into the powers of our enemy." Luca rubbed the back of her neck. "I don't understand it, Vlad. What manner of woman would turn simple folk into such ghouls?"

"The ways of the Bone Shaker are not meant to be understood," Üban answered, staring into the middle distance. "Dun-Wyrd is evil to the core." She shivered off her reverie and found her mettle. "We should move from this place, and soon. Theodora and Brennik deserve rest in less foul grounds."

"If it suits your needs, I have found another clearing a small way from here."

The three knights wheeled around.

"Abildan," Vladisal said.

How did she move so silently?

Vladisal felt Üban and Luca bristle beside her.

"Where have you been?"

"Observing." Abildan's yellow eyes and cat-like face were unreadable. "The tree-demons are returning to their master. They will trouble you no more tonight." She turned to Üban, a quirked smile on her thin lips. "And you are quite correct to speak of the mysterious ways of the Bone Shaker, as you like to call her. Dun-Wyrd is an intelligent foe."

"She doesn't seem so clever me," Üban shot back. "Bone Shaker or not, Dun-Wyrd is nothing more than a stealer of children. Her monsters failed to kill us and she underestimates her enemy."

"Failed?" Abildan's expression was filled with dark mirth. "Dun-Wyrd's intent was not to kill you - at least, not on this night."

She offered no more explanation, and Üban's eyes glared angrily. The old knight would not take much more goading before she drew her sword on the feliwyrd.

"Speak plainly, Abildan," Vladisal demanded. "Tell us what Dun-Wyrd wanted?"

"Information. She senses she is being tracked. She merely wished to see whom by."

"She... she could see us?" Luca said.

"Oh yes. Through the eyes of her army. And she had a good look at you, Sir Knight."

Luca waved the taunt away, but Vladisal could tell she was troubled by the notion of being watched through dead eyes. They all were.

"And now that she has seen us, what will she do next?"

"Nothing." Abildan shrugged. "Oh, I realise you proud Knights of Boska believe you are something to be feared, but you do not pose the threat to Dun-Wyrd that you think you do. All she sees is a band of fools on a doomed quest to rescue the son of their duchess."

"As I said," Üban growled. "She underestimates us."

"I think you are right," Abildan said, nodding. "But not in the way you believe. Your famed sense of pride is perhaps your greatest ally. Dun-Wyrd would not have considered that you might have sent a messenger for reinforcements." She chuckled. "She will think you too proud and stubborn to ask for help from others."

"But we have no help," Vladisal said. "Redheart has been gone for two days. How long before she returns with aid?"

"Hard to say. The Ulyyn are a fickle race, Sir Vladisal, dogged by code and ritual, more so than even the mighty Knights of Boska."

Vladisal exhaled an angry breath. "But the Forest Dwellers will come?"

"Oh yes. Of that I have no doubt. The likes of Dun-Wyrd are a curse upon these lands. Once convinced of her presence, the Ulyyn will not stand to let her pass."

Dief joined the group. Her usually confident demeanour had been replaced by the same moribund mood that had infected all. She gripped her hammer menacingly, as if suspecting the tree-demons of trickery and a second attack was imminent.

"Everyone is accounted for," she reported miserably.

"No one was injured?" Abildan asked.

Dief looked the feliwyrd up and down as though she was something she had stepped in, before addressing Vladisal again. "Theodora and Brennik are ready for burial – the Mother save their souls."

"Then there is no point in lingering," Vladisal said. "Assemble the women, Dief. We will bury our dead in better ground."

Without a word, Dief walked back towards the small crowd of knights and archers. With a nod to Vladisal, Luca followed her.

Abildan watched them leave with an appraising air.

"Sir Vladisal," she said, her expression curious. "I do not wish to insult your sensibilities any more than is necessary, but I have a question. Why are you wasting time burying your dead? It would be easier to simply burn their remains."

"Are you mad?" Üban erupted. "Theodora and Brennik are women of Boska!"

Abildan's smile was cruel. "I'm afraid I don't see your point."

Üban's huge frame towered over the assassin. "You are a piece of work, feliwyrd, and I've had it with your sick jokes."

"I make no joke, Sir Üban." Abildan's eyes flashed. "And your threats mean nothing to me."

"Enough," Vladisal said tiredly. "Abildan, you will lead us to the next clearing." She stood between Üban and the feliwyrd. "And we bury our dead the Boskan way."

"As you wish."

Abildan gave a mock bow, and then walked away to stand at the edge of the clearing, where she waited to lead the knights through the forest once again.

Üban's eyes were furious, her lips clamped tightly shut. She stared at Vladisal for a moment, and then stormed off in a different direction to Abildan.

Vladisal looked up at the sky. The star-filled blackness had lightened with a tinge of blue. Dawn was approaching, and it would be good to see the sun again.

"Where are you, Redheart?"

Four
Redheart

The first rays of morning filtered through the trees. Redheart's mood lightened and fatigue lifted.

The deeper into the Great Forest she travelled, the more the woodlands became touched by spring. Above, a canopy of new leaves decorated the trees. The damp floor smelled fresh and wholesome. Flowers bloomed, rich and yellow. The forest was alive with buzzing insects and wildlife scurrying through the undergrowth.

Redheart had travelled through most of the previous day and night, stopping to rest only for two or maybe three hours. Her mind was too troubled for sleep. The unfamiliarity of the territory kept her alert, the nature of her mission constantly needled her thoughts, especially when she thought of those back home in Boska. The Duchy of Mayland lay four days ride to the south of the Great Forest, and it was filled with anxious folk. Not least of all Duchess Mayland, who waited for the safe return of her son Elander.

Amidst the tranquillity of the forest, it was hard to recall the desperation that had gripped Mayland Castle a week ago. Elander had gone riding with his entourage, as he often did. There was nothing unusual about the day whatsoever, no reason to suspect that any ill was afoot. It had been a desperate farmer who came to the castle with news that the dead bodies of Elander's entourage had been found. Elander had been seen alive but draped over a horse that was being ridden hard northward by a cloaked figure.

Vladisal had been beside herself, outraged and shamed that she,

Elander's Champion, had not been there to prevent the abduction. The vow she swore to the Duchess to see her son returned unharmed was echoed by her friends – Redheart, Luca and Dief, too; and no one would have dared try to stop old Üban joining the rescue party. And so it had been. Led by Vladisal, a band of loyal knights, flying the banner of Duchess Mayland, had headed north in search of Elander.

Driven but tired and hungry, Redheart stopped to break her fast.

She sat upon the thick roots of a tree, resting her back against the sturdy trunk. Since leaving Vladisal, she had been carrying a talisman, which she laid on the ground before opening her pack, from which she took a hard oatcake and a few dried fruits. She ate while surrounded by the peace of birdsong and the ever-warming sun.

To be suited in armour, to carry a sword at her side, seemed almost an insult to the tranquillity. Up through the canopy of new leaves, she could see the sky was clear and blue. It would be a glorious day.

If any of them had thought that the abductor's plan was to hold Elander to ransom then they had been sorely mistaken. Later, it would be Abildan who revealed that their enemy was named Dun-Wyrd, and Dun-Wyrd had no interest in gold and jewels. Necromancer to some, Bone Shaker to others, she had an evil, sorcerous soul, and Redheart didn't dare to guess her reasons for taking Elander.

The trail had led the company further and further north. Along the way, they had passed three villages. Each had been deserted. There were no signs of struggles; fields and livestock were left untended, and not one single man, woman or child could be found. For all intents and purposes, the villagers had simply vanished - as had Elander's trail when it led to the northern border of Boska and the southern edge of the Great Forest.

Her breakfast finished, Redheart drank a little water from a skin, and then picked up the talisman. She studied it and ran a finger along its grooves.

Made from pale wood, the talisman was a thin and decorative piece, carved to resemble a leaf, small enough to rest in Redheart's palm. The detail in its craftsmanship was immaculate. It almost looked as though it had been plucked straight from a tree. Yet the attention to detail was not its most astounding attribute.

Gripped in Redheart's hand, the talisman grew warm when she walked in a north-easterly direction. But if she turned aside, deviated from a north-eastern path even by a little, it grew decidedly cool. For two days Redheart had been following the talisman's warmth. She trusted that it was leading her true, even if it had been a gift from an untrustworthy source.

The Great Forest covered hundreds of hectares, and Elander could have been taken in any direction. When his trail had disappeared, the Knights of Boska had become utterly lost. That had been the moment when Abildan appeared to the company.

They had all heard tell of the feliwyrd, the cat-people who were bred for dealing death. None of the knights had trusted Abildan - especially Üban who had fought against the feliwyrd in her youth – but Vladisal had recognised the need to form an alliance, however uneasy. Abildan was on a mission to assassinate Dun-Wyrd. She and the knights shared a common enemy. But even with Abildan's tracking skills, and her knowledge of the Bone Shaker's magic, the alliance was still not a strong enough force. If Dun-Wyrd's sorceries were to be defeated then reinforcements were needed, and fast.

Redheart stared at the leaf talisman.

Legends spoke of a mighty and ancient race that inhabited the Great Forest. The Forest Dwellers, many called them, but their true name was the Ulyyn. Stories of the Ulyyn were recorded in the most ancient of tomes, but it was said that even the earliest accounts had been centuries old by the time they were written down. The leaf talisman was supposedly an artefact of the Ulyyn, some kind of friendship token. Not only would it lead Redheart to this fabled race, but also grant her one favour from them. Or so Abildan had said…

She curled her fingers around the talisman.

Through all her time as a knight, Redheart had seen the very best and worst that the world had to offer; but these were strange days indeed, no matter how glorious the sun made them seem. She could not blame Vladisal for trusting Abildan – what other choice did she have? But her friend and captain blamed no one but herself for Elander's plight. She was desperate – as they all were – and the almost pleading expression that Vladisal had worn when they parted company two days ago was burned into Redheart's memory.

She would not let her friend down.

With a fresh surge of determination, Redheart got to her feet and shouldered her pack. The instant she faced northeast, the leaf talisman grew warm in her hand.

She prayed that all Abildan had said would prove to be true, that this intricately made artefact would lead her to the Ulyyn. For without their help, the Knights of Boska could not hope to overcome the power of Dun-Wyrd. The trouble was, no one knew for certain that the Forest Dwellers still existed.

Five
The Shelter of Daylight

The Knights of Boska made a simple camp beneath a cloudless blue sky.

Each woman gave silent thanks to the Mother for the arrival of a new sun. The morning light chased shadows into retreat, but not memories of the night before. Some sat around campfires, breakfasting on sparse meals; others cleaned armour or honed weapons or sharpened arrowheads. But they did not speak or jest among themselves. The aftermath of the fight lingered in the air, as palpable as the stink of Dun-Wyrd's tree-demons.

Vladisal did not sit with her women.

In silent contemplation, she stood over the fresh graves of Sir Theodora and Sir Brennik. The final resting place of these two brave knights was marked by their swords, stabbed into the ground like headstones.

Guilt was a difficult creature to ignore. There was honour in the way Theodora and Brennik had lived and died, but they had lands back in Boska, families who would deserve explanations when the company returned home. What would Vladisal tell them? That they fought bravely? That their deaths were a sacrifice their captain had been prepared to make if it led to Elander's rescue?

Weariness bit into Vladisal.

"We all mourn the dead, lass," Über said, coming alongside her. "But now you should rest and get something to eat."

"I am not hungry," Vladisal replied.

"Nor are the women, but they do as they must to keep up their strength."

Although Üban's tone was calm, Vladisal could sense the irritation simmering under the surface, and she knew the old knight still rankled from their earlier discussions. But it wasn't just her. Vladisal could sense it in Luca and Dief, too; an uncertainty that shrouded their faces each time their captain gave an order. A seed of disparity was growing within the company.

"The women are troubled," Vladisal said. "And it is more than the dark magic of last night that unsettles them."

Üban scratched at the unruly mop of her hair. "They are beginning to wonder what we are doing, Vlad. Each of them would gladly give their life to see Elander returned to Mayland Castle, but… look at them. They are forced to make camp as though simple foresters. They wear no surcoats, no house colours to be proud of, and carry no helm or shield."

"The forest is a difficult ground to navigate," Vladisal said. "Abildan said our colours would attract attention. Helms would impede our awareness, and the shields would be too cumbersome-"

"Aye – Abildan said …" Although Üban whispered, her tone cut Vladisal to silence. "These women should not be tending armour and weapons themselves, Vladisal. Their squires should be here, ensuring their masters are rested and fit for the battles to come. Yet we have left them camped on the outskirts of the Great Forest, idle and alone, as they wait for our return. And all because Abildan said? It is madness. These knights have been stripped of pride."

Vladisal glared at her. "They question my leadership?"

"No, lass!" Üban snapped. "But in this matter they wonder at your judgement, as well they should."

Honest, dependable Üban - she was nothing if not the voice of truth. Ever since the party had ridden from Mayland Castle, Vladisal had been blinkered by her determination to save Elander, to act for what she thought was the greater good. Perhaps the moment called for a little reason.

"Speak plainly, old woman," Vladisal said. "My trust in Abildan is questionable, yes?"

"I understand how you feel, Vlad, but I, perhaps best of all, know what kind of animal the feliwyrd is. She cannot be trusted. The women fear you do not see the mockery she makes of us. Abildan comes and goes as she pleases, and only the hells know what secrets she keeps."

Vladisal looked to where she had last seen Abildan, sitting upon a fallen tree at the edge of the camp. The feliwyrd had again disappeared, leaving behind her sabre, crossbow and baldric of bolts.

"All will be well when Redheart returns."

"Redheart?" Üban chuckled sourly. "I dread to think what kind of trouble she has been sent into. It doesn't sit well with me, Vlad."

"She will return."

"It's a fool's errand! That feliwyrd gives her some simple token, a talisman she says will bring the Forest Dwellers running to our aid, and..." She shook her head. "Redheart's quest is nothing more that hoping on myth and lore and fairy tales. And all the while little Elander is lost, leagues from home, in the clutches of a Bone Shaker."

Vladisal swung on the old knight, fury beating at her temples. "I will do all I can to see Elander safe. I will cut every tree in the Great Forest to the ground if need be."

"Then think! Abildan is Dun-Wyrd's countrywoman. Her kind is bred to show fealty to the Bone Shakers. So why would the Bone Shakers send her here to kill one of their own? What is it that Abildan had not told us?"

Vladisal turned away. She closed her eyes and prayed for calm, for wisdom.

"Before we left Mayland," she said with sad composure, "I swore an oath to our Duchess that I would bring her son home by any means necessary – we all did, Üban. Even you cannot deny that we need Abildan's help. She may keep her secrets, but while her foe is our foe she is not entirely untrustworthy."

"No?" Üban's face grew dark, as if remembering some past evil. "The blood of the feliwyrd runs colder than you could possibly imagine, Vladisal, and they have no need for alliances. Abildan would not be among us, she would not have shown herself, unless we serve some purpose to her quest that we do not yet know. Remember that, lass."

Üban walked away. Vladisal watched after her for a while, before gazing down at the graves of Sir Brennik and Sir Theodora.

Did this situation carry no wrong or right solution? Üban, as always, spoke only the truth as she saw it. Perhaps she was right. Perhaps it was time for Abildan to give the women of Boska some straight answers.

Six
Sacrifice

The stupidity of knights was both a source of irritation and much amusement for Abildan. They lived by such strict and confining codes of conduct that she wondered how they did not choke on their own self-righteousness.

When she had first approached Vladisal and her women, they had been camped at the southern edge of the Great Forest. They had travelled with a retinue of squires, who pampered to their every request, and tended their steeds. Garish surcoats had covered their immaculate armour, dazzling blues and reds – the colours of their cherished House Mayland. The weapons they carried were burdensome; their helms and shields ridiculously ornamented. They were like ignorant children who believed that no enemy could best their courage, for they were knights, women of Boska.

To see them now so deluded and stripped of pretence – indeed, to be the very cause of their discontent – pleased Abildan greatly. It was a lesson they were long overdue in the learning.

The feliwyrd was now a small way from the camp, following a narrow deer trail, over-grown and little-used for some time, by the looks of things. She navigated her path with cautious steps, her hand resting upon a hemp cloth sack tucked into her belt.

Ever alert to the sounds and scents around her, she could still smell the knights from the trail. The gentle breeze that rustled through the forest carried smoke from their campfires, and it was tinged with sweat and fear. Yet, the further down the trail Abildan walked, the more these aromas were clouded by the smell of something other, something inhuman - less foul than tree-demons, but far more intelligent.

Focussing her every sense, she continued on slowly.

The knights could never comprehend Abildan's reasons and actions. They clutched so fiercely to their ideals of chivalry that they had lost all appreciation for the simpler things in life - like the thrill of the hunt, for example. Though, Abildan had to admit, that old ox, Sir Üban, had the look - and the scars - of a predator. The aging fool was so long in the tooth, so full of superstition, Abildan could barely breathe without her watching. Why Vladisal kept her around when all she did was complain and argue was beyond the feliwyrd. She would have to keep an eye on that one.

The tiniest of vibrations rose up through the ground, tingling against the pads of Abildan's bare feet.

She stopped.

The vibration was accompanied by a faint clicking sound. The ears of a human would not be able to distinguish the sound from the wash of the forest, but Abildan heard it, and she knew what it came from.

With a smile, she continued along the trail.

Perhaps it was the hypocrisy of the knights that irritated her the most. They talked of duty, boasted of honour, yet in return for their dedication and fealty, they expected favour and coin from their noble masters. Abildan wondered where the chivalry of knights would be if they were stripped of their rewards. No such favours were offered by the masters of the feliwyrd.

Exacting duty, the principles of loyalty - the Boskan knights understood so little in their primitive ways. The nature of pragmatism, achieving one's goal no matter the cost, was a concept wasted on their small minds. If Vladisal's friend, Sir Redheart, was successful in bringing the Ulyyn and the knights returned Elander to his mother, safe and well, they would all be hailed as heroes in their homeland.

As for Abildan and the quest to kill Dun-Wyrd, her masters fully expected her to die in the process of this mission. Within the scheme of things, it was an insignificant price for them to pay.

She froze.

Slowly, Abildan slipped the sack from her belt. She placed it between her pointed teeth. Sharp claws slid from the ends of her fingers and toes.

The Knights of Boska were always looking to Abildan, expecting her to provide answers to questions, yet they rarely listened to her advice as though every word she spoke was a lie. They buried their dead, not burned them. They had been warned of the infectious nature of Dun-Wyrd's magic, but did not check to see if any of them had been stung by tree-demons, as Abildan suggested. They clung to honesty and openness as if the existence of the world depended on it, yet they could not see beyond their pride.

Knights were hypocrites, one and all! And Abildan knew that there were secrets hiding in their ranks, especially from their captain Vladisal. They blamed Abildan for their discontent, yet it was more a product of their captain's manufacture.

And that was the most amusing aspect concerning the stupidity of these knights: while their captain was so lost and confused, while squabbles among them were so easy to manipulate, Abildan would undoubtedly find opportunity to leave the Great Forest alive.

The ground vibrated. Clicks filled the feliwyrd's ears.

Claws sharp, she leapt forward.

A section of the trail floor flipped open like a trapdoor. A mass of legs, fangs, and a black, bloated body, sprang from a dark hole to meet the assassin. The spider was big, its body the size of Abildan's torso. And it was strong, quick as light.

With a yowl of defiance, the feliwyrd sank her claws deep into its bloated mass. Together, they fell back into the dark lair. The trapdoor closed down on them.

Seven
Pride

When Üban had been a young woman, she had travelled to a land called Mya-Siad, a nation built on desert sands and plains of sharp rock far to the east. There, she had fought in a war against a race of magickers called the Wyrd. At that time, Üban had barely finished her novitiate - a young knight ready to take on the world and all it could throw at her. She had heard the stories about the enemy's powers, but nothing could have prepared her for what she faced in that war.

The Wyrd were evil to the core. The moniker of Bone Shaker suited them well.

Üban felt every winter of her fifty-years down deep in her joints. She walked among the women, pausing here and there to praise bravery and raise spirits. But her efforts were mostly wasted. After the things they had seen last night, it was near impossible to bolster the company's moral. Each word of encouragement was met by expressions clouded by doubt.

Death was an accepted risk in a knight's duty, and the Mother only knew that Üban had seen enough of it in her time. Fighting steel with steel was one thing, but to fall beneath the vicious hunger of these tree-demons? The women were experiencing the ghosts of Üban's youth. Death had risen to mock them all, and its name was Dun-Wyrd.

Her mood sombre, Üban walked to a campfire besides which Dief lay alone upon the ground, curled on her side, snoring.

Üban let her gaze travel over the camp. The five archers sat in a group, tending arrows, talking furtively. Many of the knights sat in their undergarments, cleaning armour. Some, more cautious, remained in their

29

tarnished shells, keeping weapons sharp in preparation for whatever new horrors might spill from the forest. Even Dief, quite possibly the most fearless woman Üban had ever known, slept in her armour, clutching her mighty hammer to her chest. A light sheen of perspiration coated her face and shaven head; her face twitched as though troubled by nightmares.

Üban unbuckled her armour and beside the fire.

For centuries, the Wyrd of Mya-Siad had been trying to cultivate a future where all nations of Earth bowed to their dominance; and for centuries the nations of Earth had fought against them. The Wyrd were famed for their monstrous armies; for using dark magic to merge humans with animals, creating vicious abominations to fight for their cause. In Mya-Siad, in Üban's darkest memories, the Wyrd army had carried a very different face to that which stalked the Great Forest.

The foot-soldiers had been the caniwyrd: the sorcerous merging of human and the desert-dog known as hyena. The shortest caniwyrd stood seven feet tall, and a legion of them could march for weeks without supply lines. They found sustenance in all things, from their own bodily waste to the carrion of their dead, whose bodies still lay warm upon the battlefield. On scorching desert plains, beneath a blistering sun, Üban had spent a year fighting the caniwyrd, and she had never known a foe more remorseless and savage.

It had often seemed that the caniwyrd were an unstoppable force, who would continue to fight as long as they drew breath. But they were clumsy in their savagery, lacking the grace and tactics of trained fighting women, and that had been their one weakness. They were fearless but no match for skilled knights. However, the same could not be said for the Wyrd assassins, the warriors merged with mountain cats.

Üban's thoughts were disturbed when Luca arrived at the fire. Without a word, she unbuckled her armour and sat opposite Üban. She did not make eye contact as she cleaned her armour, or show any sign of wishing to talk. Üban respected Luca's silence, and gazed across the way, to where Vladisal still stood alone beside the graves of Theodora and Brennik.

The old knight regretted sharing harsh words with Vladisal, but she had to be told straight: Abildan and her kind were not to be trusted.

All those years ago in Mya-Siad, the older knights Üban had fought alongside had a saying: to see a feliwyrd was to see death. They stalked the night, hid in the shadows, and the only sign of their passing was the trail of blood they left behind. Just once Üban had seen a feliwyrd slain. Before it died, it killed four knights with its bare hands. They were cowardly in their ways, silent in their approach, but they were perfectionists in death, and fiercely loyal to their Bone Shaker masters.

Why Abildan should be so open in her approach to Vladisal troubled Üban. Sure enough they shared a common enemy, but Mya-Siad was five hundred leagues to the east of the Great Forest; and Mya-Siad, with its plans to dominate Earth, had started no war for over three decades.

Why was Dun-Wyrd so far from home? What had she done that could compel the Wyrd to send an assassin to kill one of their own? There was more to this situation than Abildan was saying. The bastard was up to something, something none of them could yet see.

Dief snorted loudly in her sleep, rolled over, but did not wake.

Luca shook her head. "Only she could sleep at a time like this."

Üban nodded. "You know, I once knew a guard who could sleep standing up, anytime, anywhere." She took two oatcakes from a sack of provisions. "I lost count of how many times she was flogged for napping on sentry duty."

Luca frowned. "Is this true, or another of your tall tales, old woman?"

"I saw it with my own eyes." Üban winked as she bit into an oatcake. "We called her Forty Lashes."

Luca chuckled. It was a good sound and it lifted the mood.

Dief woke. She sat up and stared around, bleary-eyed. She took a moment to remember where she was and her expression fell.

"And did the princess sleep well?" Luca asked.

Dief rubbed a hand over her head and shivered. "Damned cold," she grumbled. "All this sun and still I feel no warmth. It's as if last night has put ice in my veins."

"Aye, lass," said Üban. "We all feel that." She threw the sack to Dief. "Here, eat something."

But she shook her head and passed the sack to Luca. "I'm not hungry."

"Well there's a first," Luca said, taking a handful of dried fruits for herself. "Considering you think through your stomach, you could say I'm flabbergasted."

Dief ignored the quip. "Where's Vlad?"

Üban nodded to the solitary figure standing beside the graves.

"She should come and join us," Luca said.

"Leave her be. She needs to be alone with her thoughts a while."

"Ah, she'll be right enough once Elander is with us," Dief said. "You know Vlad - there's always hope." The big knight stood up and stamped her feet. "I need to piss," she announced.

Edward Cox

Taking her hammer with her, Dief disappeared into the trees. Üban and Luca ate their bland breakfast in silence.

Inwardly, Üban feared for her brave comrades, these good women that she had come to love as friends. Luca had been born the daughter of minor nobility. She was an intelligent girl, well-educated, a lover of poetry and history, and a firm favourite among the bachelors of Mayland. Of all the people Luca would fashion a friendship with, the colossal daughter of a common farmer was the most unlikely, yet she and Dief were as thick as thieves. The same could be said of Vladisal and Redheart, two daughters following in the footsteps of their mothers, of their grandmothers, and friends since infancy.

At the academy, these four had formed a band of foolish dreamers. Üban had been serving with them all since they were first knighted, had stood witness when they swore fealty to House Mayland. Often had been the time when the old knight berated them for their high-jinx escapades, yet inwardly she had enjoyed their spiritedness, the passion of their youth. She had come to think of herself as the teacher who helped a quartet of fools grow into honourable women.

There had been no bitterness when Vladisal rose above her friends, above Üban, to become a captain of knights and Elander's champion. It had surprised no one; Vladisal always stuck out from the pack, a thoughtful and logical woman, dedicated to good and honest ways. But now, unbeknownst to Luca and Dief, Vladisal was lost.

"Why do you think Dun-Wyrd wants Elander?" Luca said as she settled back in the sunshine. "I have read of the Wyrd's evil nature, but also that they are calculating, that their cruelty is never for cruelty's sake alone."

"You've read right." Üban scratched her head. "I wonder at Dun-Wyrd's purpose myself. But I remain as mystified as you, Luca."

"It makes no sense. What possible reason could an innocent child serve a Bone Shaker?"

"Let us hope that we do not find out. And trust to Redheart. All will be well when she returns."

The uncertainty on Luca's face mirrored that which Üban was hiding.

"I wonder how Redheart's faring," Luca said. "She's been gone an awful long time. Too long for my liking."

Dief returned and sat down heavily beside the fire. She picked up the water-skin and drank deeply.

"Can't stomach food," she muttered, wiping her mouth, "but I have a thirst that even an ocean could not slake." She stoppered the skin and threw it to Luca.

"Perhaps you're ailing." Luca smiled. "Maybe you've caught a dose of the sniffles."

"Don't be an idiot! I'm as strong as an ox."

Luca shrugged and drank.

Dief looked around. "So, what do we plan next?"

"We wait." Üban's expression grew dark. "Until Abildan points us in the right direction again."

Dief made a noise not unlike a growl and pointed to where Abildan's sabre and crossbow lay against the fallen tree. "I see its belongings, but not the monster itself."

"Some of the women saw her move off into the trees an hour or so ago," Luca said. "I tell you, Üban, they do not like her presence. They wonder if she has placed some spell over Vlad."

Dief slapped the head of her hammer, as though patting a dog. "She'll do no harm to us, not while I have this in my hand," she promised.

"Don't be so sure," Üban warned. "There is no spell upon Vladisal, at least none of the feliwyrd's casting. There is sense in using Abildan's guidance, but Vlad is blinded to the assassin's nature. I fear to think what it would do to her if Abildan turns against us and Elander perishes."

"Then we will stay on our guard at all times," Dief said.

"After last night, I don't think any woman here would dream of doing any different." Luca pursed her lips. "Abildan's a handy sort to have around in a fight, though. Did you see her last night?" She gave a low whistle. "I thought I was quick with a sabre, but she was something else."

"She's certainly that, lass," Üban said sourly. She nodded towards the tree line. "Look…"

Abildan had returned. She walked across the camp wearing her usual supercilious expression, paying no mind to the glares from the women around her. Over her shoulder, she carried a bulging cloth sack that looked heavy.

"Where's she been all this time?" Dief wondered.

Abildan reached the fallen log where she had left her belongings. She dumped the sack on the ground, sat upon the log, and then produced a small and slim box of dark wood from beneath her shirt. She opened it and studied its contents.

"See that box she holds?" Luca said. "I've seen her looking at it before. I wonder what's inside."

"Perhaps we should ask her," Dief said menacingly. "My hammer will get some straight answers."

Luca, so often the voice of reason to Dief's hot-headedness, agreed with her friend this time. "That's not a bad idea," she said, looking at Üban. "You know, I have read much about the Great Forest and the Ulyyn, and the more I think upon it, the less Abildan is making sense. What do you think, old woman? It can't hurt to ask a few questions."

"Wait," Üban said softly.

Across the camp, Vladisal had turned from the graves, and was staring at Abildan. She then strode towards the assassin purposefully.

"Let Vlad have her turn first." The old knight gazed across the fire at Luca. "For the meantime, tell me what you have read about the Forest Dwellers."

Eight
Hidden Lands

The morning wore on, the sun climbed higher in the sky, and Redheart became aware that the warmth of the talisman was now accompanied by a faint vibration that tingled against her palm.

She hoped this was a sign that her destination was close. The sameness of the forest made her feel lost, and if she did not keep faith in the talisman's magic, then she would swear she walked in circles.

Redheart marched on, eating as she walked. She couldn't afford to waste time resting again, no matter how fatigued she felt.

Soon, the forest began to thicken. The canopy of leaves grew so dense that sunlight barely filtered through. Here, in this shade, the air grew decidedly cooler. Beneath her armour, Redheart's sweating body found welcome relief from the drop in temperature.

In the distance, a woodpecker hammered upon a tree. The vibrations of the leaf talisman seemed in tune with the sound.

The Ulyyn were such a mysterious race. It was said they were the last of the Elder Born - the first children who the Mother God birthed onto Her Earth. Yet no one had seen the Ulyyn in many years, not during Redheart's lifetime, nor her mother's. Some believed they had died out; others that they had become clandestine creatures who preferred to live isolated in their woodland sanctum. Either way, the domain of the Ulyyn lay somewhere inside the Great Forest, and its name was in Uljah - a great and fabled city without compare, legend said. And Redheart, on the word of a feliwyrd, was trying to find it.

She had to keep faith that this wooden artefact, so intricately carved into the likeness of a leaf, was steering her towards the city of the Forest Dwellers.

Redheart stopped in her tracks.

A short way ahead, the forest became so thick that it was hard to see a path through. Trees stood closer together; the undergrowth and bracken grew higher and denser, filling the space between the trees like a solid weave knitted from sharp thorns and twisting vines. The blockade continued to the left and right without end as far as Redheart could see, as sturdy-looking as a wall of Mayland Castle.

Her shoulders slumped.

The way was blocked. The forest had placed a dead end before her, and she suspected that an entire company of foresters armed with keen axes would need days to cut a path through to the other side. But there was so little time to spare as it was. Who knew how long it would take her to walk around this impassable area? For all she knew, it might stretch all the way through the Great Forest.

Daunted, Redheart sighed and turned away from the wall. Immediately, the leaf talisman grew cooler and stopped vibrating. Only when she faced straight on to the dense foliage did the talisman's warmth return and its vibrations resume.

With a frown, Redheart stepped closer to the forest wall. The talisman approved. She peered into the thickness. There was little light inside the area, only enough to offer slight hues of deep green and dark brown. Perhaps there was a way through after all; maybe the talisman was telling her of some hidden path that she could not yet see.

Treading sideways, Redheart moved a little to her right. The talisman's magic grew faint in her hand. Three steps to the left, and the magic grew strong again - and stronger still with every step.

She kept moving until the talisman vibrated so fiercely it stung her skin. Just at the point where she thought its heat would burn her, there came a sudden rustling within the foliage that made her flinch. She stepped back and watched in amazement.

A section of the forest parted, as though drapes were being dragged open by thorny fingers to be tied off with tight ropes of vine. To Redheart's astonishment, a circular tunnel was revealed, leading into impassable area.

"What magic is this?" she whispered.

The talisman had ceased vibrating. Its heat had become a gentle warmth that pulsed against Redheart's palm as though egging her onward with its rhythm. The opening beckoned.

Was this the entrance to Uljah?

Gingerly, she stepped into the tunnel. Its height was shorter than an average woman, and she had to stoop as she walked. Light came from luminous fungus growing in clusters upon the wall. Dusty cobwebs hanging thick and silvery stroked her face. With one hand clutching the talisman, Redheart gripped the pommel of her sword with the other.

The path sloped downward until it surely burrowed beneath the forest floor. A cool breeze came from somewhere ahead, bringing with it lush and sweet scents. Before long, the tunnel's end came into sight, a circular opening bright with glorious sunshine.

Redheart froze. Her heartbeat quickened.

A figure had appeared at the opening, limned by sunshine. It stood still for a moment, staring down the tunnel at the Boskan knight, before rushing away.

"Wait!" Redheart called.

She gave chase.

Reaching the end of the tunnel, she tripped and stumbled into some kind of depression that served as a bowl-like clearing. The floor was covered in soft, green moss, decorated by fallen leaves of many hues and colours. High above, the tree line swept around to encircle the clearing.

Redheart's eyes found the one she chased.

It stood several paces away, but what manner of creature it was Redheart could only guess.

A clear head and shoulders taller than most women, it was painfully thin yet powerful looking. Its skin had the texture of smooth bark, and its wide hands ended in long and pointed fingers, like sharpened sticks. Patches of moss acted as hair on its head and a beard on a face that had no ears, no nose, but a mouth that hung open like a woody hollow. And its eyes - eyes that stared at Redheart so dispassionately - were tawny orbs that never blinked.

Was this one of the Ulyyn?

"I am Sir Redheart of House Mayland." She showed the creature the leaf talisman. "I'm on a mission of mercy."

A noise came from the creature's mouth, like the moaning of the wind. Two vines unfurled from its back, rising high like snakes writhing in the air.

Redheart knew a threat when she saw one. Her hand moved to her sword. "I mean you no harm," she warned.

The creature sprang forward.

Before Redheart could draw her weapon, one of the vines lashed out with dazzling quickness. She yelled in pain as its tip whipped across her face. Fire spread through her veins with such speed and agony that she fell onto her back. The world spun into darkness.

Nine
Trust

Her mood delicately poised between despair and fury, Vladisal strode towards Abildan. The feliwyrd sat on a fallen log, studying the contents of a small box. As soon as the knight's shadow fell across her, she snapped the box shut and placed it beneath her shirt.

"Sir Vladisal." The assassin didn't look up. "Something is troubling you?"

Vladisal's eyes fixed on the hemp cloth sack sitting on the ground. It was tied at the neck and obviously well stuffed. "What's that?" she demanded.

Abildan looked up. "A sack."

Vladisal bristled. "What's in it?"

"Something dead."

Although her tone didn't hold any mockery, Abildan's expression remained indifferent, uncaring, as though the disdain she incurred from the women of Boska meant nothing to her.

Vladisal scoffed and looked over the camp. "How long before you find the Bone Shaker's lair?"

"I already have. It's no more than three hours walk from here."

Vladisal was taken aback. "Why didn't you say so before?"

"Calm yourself, Sir Knight."

"No." Vladisal's anger rose. "If Dun-Wyrd is truly within a few hours walk, then we leave now and both our quests can come to an end."

"Without reinforcements at our side?" Abildan clucked her tongue. "Not your best idea, Sir Vladisal. Look around you. Your women are tired and frightened. They need rest."

Vladisal swallowed her anger. Most knights were indeed trying to rest. Some watched their captain's exchange with Abildan - most notably Üban, Luca and Dief.

"Your friend Redheart must be given every chance to bring the Ulyyn to us," Abildan said. "And please understand - Dun-Wyrd does not perceive you as a threat. But like all her kind, she is ever the pragmatist. She will no doubt see an opportunity to add you and your knights to her army. And she is quite content waiting for you to come to her."

"Then what of you?" Vladisal said with a tired and resigned edge. "What kind of threat does a Bone Shaker perceive in a feliwyrd?"

Abildan's yellow eyes glinted. "It would have given us an advantage had Dun-Wyrd not known I was among you. But I have no doubt that she saw me during the battle last night, through the eyes of her tree-demons. Had you not acted so rashly, Sir Vladisal, I might have remained your secret weapon."

Vladisal averted her gaze, feeling a momentary pang of shame. No, she should never have led such a reckless charge, but what was done was done, and she would learn by her mistake. She would not be haunted by it.

Abildan was looking past Vladisal, to the graves of Theodora and Brennik, her eyes narrowed shrewdly. "The disease of Dun-Wyrd's magic shows no mercy."

Crouching, Vladisal picked up two stones and rattled them in a loose fist. "I want your word, Abildan. I want your word that when the time comes, you will do all you can to help us save Elander."

"I will give you no such thing," Abildan replied with a chuckle. "My duty is to ensure that Dun-Wyrd ceases to breathe. The son of Duchess Mayland is your responsibility. He means nothing to me. Do not ever doubt it."

Vladisal stopped rattling the stones and glared at the feliwyrd.

Abildan raised a hand for calm, and when she spoke, her tone was exasperated. "When we first met, you had no idea that you pursued a Wyrd. You had lost Elander and did not know how to proceed. You decided that this alliance was the best way forward, Vladisal, and you had no need to hear my promises back then."

"Back then we were not fighting tree-demons!"

Abildan threw her head back and laughed heartily, revealing pointed canines. "And you blame me for this? No, no, Sir Knight, I explained what manner of enemy you faced before you agreed to an alliance. And you knew what kind of animal I was. If you hoped that your chivalrous virtues would rub off on me, then I am happy to disappoint. All I have given you is a chance to save Elander. How you use that chance is entirely up to you."

Vladisal took a calming breath. Just for once, she wished Abildan would speak with a civil tongue; show some degree of the humanity and compassion that would make Üban and the rest of the knights see that their captain's trust was not misplaced. Or was it herself Vladisal was trying to convince?

She stood up and threw the stones aside. "Why did they send you here, Abildan? Why do the Wyrd wish to kill one of their own?"

Abildan cocked her head to one side. "My masters have given me no explanation of Dun-Wyrd's crimes against Mya-Siad. I'm merely following orders."

"Ah, but you are no fool. What do you suspect are her crimes? Why do you think Dun-Wyrd has come to the Great Forest? What does she plan for Elander?"

Abildan paused for a moment, calculating. "Answer me this - if we had every fact, every piece of information that answered all questions to everyone's satisfaction, what difference would it make? Would you and I not still be here, serving our masters as we must?"

"Understanding duty can push a knight harder to succeed," Vladisal said proudly. "It gives us a sense of belonging."

"An interesting albeit pointless philosophy."

"I'm not here to discuss philosophy, Abildan. Talk straight, damn you!"

Cat-like eyes narrowed. "You throw question after question at me, as though I am yours to command, and then you demand straight talk? If we truly share an alliance, isn't trust and truth a mutual commodity?"

When she received no reply, Abildan snorted and shook her head. "You knights share much in common with the Ulyyn, Sir Vladisal. They too demand honesty while harbouring secrets of their own. Your armour shines with chivalrous virtue, yet beneath you are selective with whom you show courtesy, and your prejudices are telling. You would offer me nothing, while expecting everything in return."

"Think what you will." Vladisal sneered. "I am not the one serving masters of cruelty. I offered you my hand of respect, Abildan. It was you who chose to spit upon it with your mocking ways."

"You would speak to me of respect?" The yellow of Abildan's eyes flashed angrily. "You could not even give me thanks after I saved your life." She leant forward and her voice dropped to a whisper. "I could have left you, you know. I could have let Dun-Wyrd's monsters strip the flesh from your bones. But I didn't because I uphold our alliance, Sir Knight." She leaned back and sniffed in disdain. "The truth is the Ulyyn are better than you. At least they are honourable enough to respect a life-debt, without prejudice."

The feliwyrd's words were like a slap across Vladisal's face. Her pride evaporated as she thought of the battle the previous night, of her tangle with the tree-demons. In doing so, she came to realise that without Abildan's quick blade, Üban, Luca and Dief would never have reached their captain in time to save her.

"You're right," Vladisal admitted. "You saved my life. I should have thanked you for that."

"Think nothing of it." Abildan averted her gaze as though embarrassed. "For one of your own kind, you would not struggle with your words. But for someone like me - a servant of cruel masters, as you say - I can understand how your appreciation might run dry."

"Perhaps you are right," Vladisal said. "But from now on, I will push our differences aside. I consider myself indebted to you."

"Truly?"

"I give you my word." Vladisal managed a smile. "Let us honour this alliance by sharing the truth with each other."

Abildan seemed genuinely surprised by this statement. When she next spoke, there was uncertainty in her voice. "Then... you wouldn't mind if I asked some questions of my own?"

"Please, ask what you will."

The feliwyrd looked around to ensure that no other was in earshot. "You are Elander's champion, yes? You and the boy are close?"

Vladisal nodded.

"You talk often? He shares his secrets with you?"

"Yes."

"Does Elander have nightmares?"

Vladisal frowned. "Excuse me?"

"Does he see things in his dreams so disturbing that he pisses the bed?"

Vladisal clenched her teeth. "What is this?"

"I mean no disrespect," Abildan replied quickly. "Perhaps I should rephrase the question." A slow smile curled her thin lips. "In recent times, has Elander been speaking in a manner that might be construed as witchery to you Boskans?"

"Mind your words, Abildan," Vladisal warned. "It is the son of a noble house you are mocking, and I will not tolerate such baseless accusations."

"Baseless? The boy has had no visions of the future? He does not dream of events that come to pass?"

Vladisal's face twitched.

"Ah," said Abildan. "Your expressions tell me all I need to know, Sir Knight." She became hard and mocking again. "Elander has the Sight, as you call it, yes?"

Vladisal panicked. What if the women overheard? "Hold your tongue," she hissed.

But Abildan did no such thing, and continued with an air of triumph. "And so we come to understand why dear Elander is of such interest to Dun-Wyrd. The boy has the Sight, Vladisal. There is magic in his veins, magic which a Bone Shaker can use to do many terrible things."

Vladisal's hands balled into fists.

Abildan sat back and folded her arms across her chest. "There, Sir Knight – one of your questions is answered, and it was you who kept the truth secret all along. Doesn't it feel good to honour our alliance, to trust each other?"

"Damn you, Abildan."

"Never fear, your secret is safe with me – for now." She slipped off the log and, using the hemp cloth sack and its contents as a pillow, laid on the ground with her back to the Boskan captain. "I need to rest and gather my thoughts. I suggest you do the same."

Vladisal stared at her for a moment. Dread dominating her, she turned and walked away, suddenly filled with a desire to find a quiet place, far from everyone, where she could order her mind.

The voice of Abildan followed her.

"Prepare yourself, Sir Vladisal. Now you've admitted to your little secret, the stakes have changed. Sir Redheart has until tomorrow morning to return. Whether the Ulyyn are with us or not, we march for Dun-Wyrd's lair come the next sun."

Ten
Uljah

She knew her name was Redheart. She was a Knight of Boska. She remembered that she was on a quest to save the son of her duchess. She recalled parting company with her friends from Mayland. But her thoughts were hazy, jumbled, disorganised. There was a grey area in her mind, like a hole in her memory, tormented by dreams of monstrous serpents spitting venom at her face.

Through muddled senses, Redheart understood that she was outside. In a forest. Birds trilled. Insects clicked and buzzed.

She tried to open her eyes, just a crack, but blazing sunshine forced them shut. Her tongue was too dry to moisten cracked lips. Her face felt swollen and sore. Skin burned, drenched in hot sweat, prickling as though the embers of a fire lay upon it. She so dearly wished to tear free of her armour and feel the soothing kiss of the forest breeze upon her body. But Redheart was too weak to move.

From the swirling cloud of confusion, an image drifted to the surface. A leaf. It represented an ancient race. Didn't it?

The answer never came. Her mind once again spiralled down to that grey area where great, venomous serpents waited. And Redheart decided that she was dying…

Shivering like the harshest winter had set inside her body, Redheart felt the sensation of rising. A smooth, gradual lifting, which convinced her that her spirit was ascending into the heavens and the loving arms of the Mother God.

But the movement was accompanied by a creaking sound, as though she hung from the end of a complaining rope. The ascent stopped. Gentle swaying. Creaking.

Movement.

Whispers.

Knuckles rapped sharply upon the hard shell of Redheart's breastplate. She groaned, unable to open her eyes. Quick and rough hands removed her armour. The rank scent of her body filled her nostrils as her gambeson was pulled free. Warm sunshine eased her shivering.

Whoever had stripped Redheart naked did not speak, and busied themselves smothering her face with a foul-smelling salve. It stung bitterly. She tried to struggle, but her arms, already weakened, were easily restrained. A hot and sour brew was poured into her mouth. It burned the back of Redheart's throat as she gagged and swallowed.

The fire in her veins dulled instantly. The soft call of peaceful sleep beckoned. Just as Redheart succumbed to the call, she heard the sound of creaking rope and felt herself rising once again…

She remembered her quest to find the Ulyyn. She remembered being attacked by a strange, vicious plant-creature…

Redheart's eyes snapped open. Her vision was blurred. She sat bolt upright.

She touched a hand to her face, feeling the line of a weeping sore that began from just below her right eye and ran diagonally down across her nose and cheek, ending at the bottom of her right jaw line. Despite the wound, her fever had passed, the poison cleaned from her blood, and she felt healthy enough.

Her eyes gained focus on the wooden bars of the cramped cage that imprisoned her.

Redheart's armour and sword were gone. She had been dressed in a simple gown of a greenish brown material that seemed to be woven from moss and leaves. It was light and soft against her skin. She sat upon a thin mattress of the same material, which formed the floor of the cage.

She tested the bars of her prison. The wood was hard and sturdy, held secure by thick ropes of vine.

Redheart looked up through the bars overhead. The sky was clear and blue, and the sun was well past its zenith. The cage was suspended from another, thicker vine rope. It ran through a wooden pulley connected to a sturdy frame, and coiled around a heavy drum spool.

Redheart adjusted her position, and the cage swayed a little. The rope creaked ominously.

The cage hung before a wall of what seemed to be thick, gnarled bark. An arched doorway had been cut into it, smaller than the average doorway. It was too dark inside to see what lay beyond. Redheart lifted the mattress to see what lay below. There was a wooden platform, and the cage hung over a large hole cut into it. Through the hole, she could see another platform with another hole cut into it. There seemed to be yet another beneath that.

She looked back to the bark wall, lips pursed. How many levels did this structure have? How high was her prison? She twisted her position to look behind her.

Her breath caught.

"By the Mother."

A forest of behemoth trees sprawled before her.

Struck by a sudden wave of vertigo, Redheart gripped the bars tightly.

By what law of nature trees could grow so huge, she could not guess. Greater than the tallest, widest towers of the mightiest castles, they were too numerous to count. Each was ringed by many levels of platforms, held aloft by huge, leafless branches, starting at the very tops of the trees and reaching all the way down to the forest floor.

Upon these platforms, Redheart saw hundreds of figures going about their day, disappearing and appearing through many arched doorways. Perhaps like the buildings of a city, these trees serve as homes for families and businesses alike. It was easy to imagine chambers and stairwells carved inside these impossibly monstrous trunks.

Was this the fabled city of the Forest Dwellers? Was this Uljah?

Redheart looked at bark wall before the cage, realising at once that the wall was the trunk of yet another tree so huge that she could not see around it.

A noise came from beyond the darkened doorway. Two guards emerged, both carrying spears.

Naked and vulnerable, Redheart shied from them.

Shorter than Redheart by at least a head and neck, their armour almost doubled as camouflage, the same colour and texture as the thick and gnarled bark of the enormous trunk behind them. The skin of their small, delicate faces was tinged with green and brown, as was their unruly hair. Everything about these guards seemed to represent some aspect of the forest, especially their small autumnal eyes that regarded the Boskan knight with dispassion. They stood on either side of the doorway, holding their spears menacingly.

Redheart knew she was looking upon the Ulyyn, and felt a surge of hope.

She tried to speak, but her throat would only release a dry croak. The leaf talisman! If she showed it to them they would surely recognise that she had come in peace. But in that moment Redheart realised that the leaf talisman, along with her armour and sword, was gone.

A shadow fell across the cage. The two guards snapped to attention. A cry came from above.

Redheart looked up as the shadow descended on her. It carried the slow beat of huge wings, and she raised her hands as wind buffeted her through the bars of the cage. A great form landed gracefully upon the platform with long talons clicking and scratching at the wood.

Redheart stared in wonder.

She had heard tales of the giant hawks that nested in the mountain ranges at the northern edge of the Great Forest, but knew of nobody who had actually seen one. The great bird's feathers were thick and golden-brown, and its beak looked big and powerful enough to remove Redheart's head with a single peck.

An Ulyyn woman slid down from the giant hawk's back. The guards bowed then flanked her as she approached the cage and regarded Redheart with narrowed eyes and intolerant body language.

She wore robes of the forest, and a torc of wood around her neck decorated with lines of gold and red. Her earth coloured hair was not unruly like the guards', but styled into a topknot. She wore an expression on her small, green-tinged face that clearly represented simmering anger.

She spoke to Redheart in a language that was utterly alien. A series of harsh clicks and grunts came from her mouth, followed an expectant, demanding glare.

Redheart swallowed and found enough moisture to utter a hoarse whisper. "I cannot understand you," she said. "I come here in peace."

The Ulyyn paused a moment, before producing an item from the folds of her robe. It was the leaf talisman.

"You. Have this." She spoke the words clumsily, with a curious accent.

"Yes," Redheart said. "It helped me find you. It was gifted to me."

"Gifted." It was hard to tell if she spoke a question or an accusation. "Where monster?"

Redheart shook her head. "Forgive me, but you are making no sense."

The Ulyyn shoved the talisman back into her robes with an angry, snappish movement. She bared her teeth and restated her question. "Where?"

Redheart didn't know how to reply, and opened her hands helplessly.

With a snarl, the Ulyyn snatched a spear from the nearest guard. She thrust it through the bars of the cage. Redheart froze as the point rested against her throat. Even though the spearhead was made of wood, it was keen and sharp against her skin.

"Wait!" Redheart pleaded. "Evil has come to your forest. You must hear me!"

"Yes," the Ulyyn hissed. "I hear. Words you speak." She applied a little more pressure behind the spear, and Redheart felt its blade nick the skin of her neck. "Where monster?" she shouted. "Where Abildan?"

Eleven
Eavesdropper

Abildan was thinking about her homeland.

Mya-Siad was a long way from the Great Forest. She had lost count of how many weeks had passed since her hunt for Dun-Wyrd had begun. She missed the dry heat of the desert, the smell of scorched sand. She longed to see the great towers and plazas of Siadan City, where the streets were full of markets, and the twisting back lanes were full of shadows and danger. The beauty of the Great Forest was wasted on the feliwyrd. Her senses were stifled by it.

At the edge of the Boskan camp, Abildan sat on the highest branch of a sturdy tree, far from the petty irritation of Sir Vladisal's knights. Evening had already dulled the sky, and all was quiet, although the edgy and sombre atmosphere still hung over the camp, as it did over all the Great Forest. There was also an air of boredom among the knights, a restlessness spawned by an entire day of inaction. They felt their time was wasted by resting idly. Abildan was enjoying the calm while it lasted, for she knew what the night would bring.

Up on her high perch, she reached inside her shirt and pulled free a small, slim box of dark wood.

The interior of the box was padded with purple velvet. Upon the padding lay a single crossbow bolt of unique design. It was expertly crafted, perfectly weighted. The shaft was thin and made from black metal; the flight had been fashioned from the grey feathers of a desert hawk. The head held a conical shape, made as a sharp spiralling blade of silver that caught the fading sunlight quite majestically. It was a perfect weapon for a perfect assassin.

Abildan looked up into the sky. The first stars had appeared in the deepening blue. Not long now.

The Wyrd of Mya-Siad believed in one inevitable truth: that the day would come when all the world would be covered in their glory. For generations, centuries, the Wyrd had been studying timelines, manipulating and cultivating the future. The women of Boska thought them savage, evil, and their simple-minded superstitions called them Bone Shakers.

The knights had no understanding of the greater science of Mya-Siad; they could not fathom the intricacies of a nation's plans that would one day lead to a future where every country and race of Earth would bend to the rule of the Wyrd. And the Wyrd would kill anyone who stood in their way, even their own kind.

Abildan ran her finger along the bolt's spiralling blade. Symbols were engraved along the flat of it, written when the silver was still hot. The meaning of the symbols was not taught to so low a subject as the feliwyrd, but Abildan understood their purpose. She supposed that they formed a message of a kind, a magical battle cry from Mya-Siad to the renegade Dun-Wyrd.

She had spoken the truth when she told Sir Vladisal that she did not know why her masters wanted their countrywoman dead. Not so long ago, Dun-Wyrd had been an esteemed hierarch of Mya-Siad. Her fall from grace and eventual death warrant had been as much a surprise as a mystery. But although it was not Abildan's place to question, the situation was beginning to make a little more sense, especially in light of Vladisal's confirmation of Elander's gift.

Voices reached her ears.

Four knights had moved away from the camp. They came to stand beneath Abildan's high perch, unaware of her presence. Keeping silent, the feliwyrd smiled as their hushed voices rose up to her ears.

"What's the meaning of this?" Sir Vladisal said.

"We need to speak with you alone," old Üban replied in a gruff voice.

Sir Luca remembered a little respect for her captain, and her tone was kinder. "Just hear us out, Vlad. This needs to be said."

The colossal one, Sir Dief, said nothing and stood holding her hammer across her chest.

Vladisal sighed heavily.

"I don't need to air my feelings on chasing faeries and shadows," Üban said. "I think you know my frustrations well enough by now."

"Indeed."

"Then let us suppose that Redheart is successful in finding the Ulyyn,

49

and ask ourselves a question. Why should the Forest Dwellers help a group of knights running around their lands like fools, especially when there's a feliwyrd in their company?"

"Üban-"

"Listen to her, Vlad," Sir Luca urged. "She speaks for Dief and me also."

Dief grunted agreement. Abildan studied the big knight. In the fading light, there seemed to be a waxy, unhealthy sheen on Dief's pale face.

"Then speak." Vladisal said in a low voice laced with suspicion.

"The Ulyyn are lovers of nature," Luca said. "They believe that every creature has a divine right to follow the natural progression of life, unhindered, without manipulation. In this, the Ulyyn and the Wyrd do not make easy bedfellows."

Abildan conceded the point with a slow, silent nod.

Luca continued. "Why would the likes of Abildan possess a talisman of the Ulyyn, when the feliwyrd are in every way an abomination to them? Such a perversion of life is an insult to their beliefs, Vlad, and they would kill her on sight. It makes no sense that they would give her that talisman."

Vladisal was quiet for a moment. "It also makes little sense that Mya-Siad would send an assassin to kill a Wyrd, but Abildan is-"

"Will you stop defending that bastard animal!" Üban hissed. "Abildan is hiding something from us, and it might make the difference between Elander living or dying!"

Abildan nicked her finger on the crossbow bolt's blade. She licked the blood away.

"Please, Vlad, will you listen to your friends?" Dief sounded tired, like her voice came from a raw and dry throat. "No one among us is learned in history and lore above Luca, and there is more to what she knows."

Luca said, "If Abildan has any kind of history with the Ulyyn - which seems doubtful, but if it is there - then it cannot be good history. We are the ones following her, Vlad. Why would the Ulyyn see us as anything other than the enemy?"

"But that's a small matter," Üban said coldly. "Abildan has lied to you, Vlad - lied to us all. Whatever that talisman is, we can be entirely assured that we or Redheart do not need it to find the Ulyyn.

"Tell her, Luca," Dief croaked.

Luca ran a hand through her lank hair. "Legends of the Forest Dwellers are mixed and varied, but all the histories I have read agree on this - the Ulyyn are in tune with the forest. They literally feel through the trees, the roots in the ground, the very earth, and they can detect when intruders tread upon their lands. The Great Forest is their realm, Vlad.

They would feel our presence."

Vladisal looked uncertain. "You're saying that they already know we are here?"

"No," Üban growled. "She's saying that if the Ulyyn still existed at all then they would have attacked us by now, talisman or not."

The following silence was heavy.

Vladisal swore.

Abildan shook her head, closed the box, and slid it back under her shirt.

"Actually, that's only half true," she said, before jumping down to land gracefully beside Sir Üban.

All four knights took an involuntary step back.

Abildan cast a yellow-eyed glare on Dief. "Your friend might be learned in history, Sir Knight, but the trouble with history is that it lacks experience, always written by those who were never there."

She turned to Luca. "The truth is, the Ulyyn are hypocrites. With one hand they respect and nurture life above all other things, yet with the other they would take it from you as if it were worthless."

She looked to Vladisal. "Yes, the Ulyyn are in tune with their environment, but even their magic cannot encompass the Great Forest in its entirety. No. They feel the land only to the borders of their city. The Ulyyn do not detect us because we do not stand in Uljah, and, more importantly, nor does Dun-Wyrd."

Lastly, Abildan turned to old Üban. "Your suspicions are quite correct. I know many, many things that I would never tell you. As for being a liar, I prefer the term pragmatist."

Üban's hand rested on her sword. "Your words have little to trust in them, Abildan."

"And we're sick of your games," Dief said.

"Sick?" Abildan peered into the big knight's wan face. "Yes, you do seem a little unwell."

Dief bristled - eager to turn her hammer on the small assassin.

"Enough," Vladisal ordered. "You know there is truth in what Luca has said, Abildan. Tell us, what is the talisman? Does it truly come from the Ulyyn?"

Abildan clamped her jaw. To prattle so was an unnecessary waste of time. But she could not face Dun-Wyrd alone, and if these knights were to prove useful, then they needed to act with a clear head, a clear conscience. Vladisal's closest friends needed a reason to trust their captain's judgement, and if they fell in line, so would the rest of the women of Boska.

Unquestioningly. The feliwyrd could see that this would not happen now until she threw them a bone, as it were.

"Very well," she said. "I came to the Great Forest a long time ago. Again on the orders of Mya-Siad, but with a very different quest. Regardless, be assured that the talisman was given to me by the Ulyyn. It was a gift. Of sorts."

Cutting through Üban's disbelieving scoff and Luca's dubious reaction, Vladisal said, "For what reason? You heard Luca - the Ulyyn would not tolerate a feliwyrd so easily."

"You're right," said Abildan. "But the Ulyyn do like to complicate matters for themselves."

She frowned at the four demanding expressions, lingering a moment on Dief's, before sighing and looking to the darkening sky.

"It's growing late, but…" Abildan grinned. "Perhaps there is time enough for a tale to be told…"

Twelve
Abildan and the Ulyyn

Far in the east, the desert planes of Mya-Siad sprawled beneath a harsh sun and bitter moon. There, surrounded by leagues of unforgiving sands, stood Siadan City, the greatest city on Earth, home to tens of thousands.

The southern edge of Siadan City sat in the shadows of the Dead Mountains, a vast range of black and sharp rock whose summits reached high into the bleached sky. Carved into the faces of the Dead Mountains were the dark towers of the Wyrd, who ruled over their subjects with an uncompromising fist.

The citizens never questioned the hierarchs of Mya-Siad. Night and day they felt the all-seeing gazes from the dark towers, as though a great bird of prey ever loomed over them. The magic of the Wyrd was potent and terrible, but they ruled their country well, and had brought much prosperity to a desert nation over the centuries. The citizens respected that and, as harsh as their masters were, they knew the Wyrd worked tirelessly to ensure Mya-Siad's greatness, to perfect every aspect of society, and, most especially, to govern the shape of the future.

Far beneath the black towers, in the very belly of the Dead Mountains, the Wyrd kept their favourite pets chained to the floors of lightless caverns.

The oracwyrd.

They had once been human, yet with their withered, useless bodies, and colourless, blind eyes, the oracwyrd could hardly be described as such now. After years of dreaming in clouds of opium smoke, after decades of suffering the torments of magic poisoning, their minds had grown beyond the need for physical bodies, beyond the designs of the cursed Mother God. The oracwyrd were spirits of prescience. Their dreams were bright, alive, and their visions were far-seeing.

Without reward or respite, the oracwyrd dreamed of infinite timelines, searching for every possible future where the rule of Mya-Siad had come to dominate Earth. The Wyrd studied what their pets saw, and learned how that future could be achieved. They recognised crucial events which had to pass, and what obstacles needed to be removed. And remove them the Wyrd did, with merciless precision.

Often, the oracwyrd gave their masters a name - a name of one who would in some way hinder the quest for dominance. At such times the Wyrd did not hesitate to unleash their most deadly assassins. And the feliwyrd rarely failed in their tasks…

Deep in the Great Forest, shafts of summer sunshine speared through a verdant canopy, down onto a small figure, half-human, half-cat.

Abildan the feliwyrd sat cross-legged upon the leafy floor, only vaguely aware of the birdsong twittering around her. In the hazy heat, she stared ahead to where the forest had become dense and impenetrable. Her journey from Mya-Siad to the Great Forest had comprised many long weeks of hard travelling; and now, to the untrained eye, it seemed that Abildan's journey had come to a dead end.

But where others would see tree and brush grown into wild, impassable woodland over the years, the feliwyrd saw a construct, a work of magical engineering, a wall that protected the borders of a city called Uljah where the Ulyyn dwelt. She could attempt to hack and slash her way through, but she would never cut a path to the land beyond, not if she spent the remainder of her life trying to do so. No. There was only one way to enter the forest city.

On the ground before Abildan lay a doe. Dead, its throat torn out by sharp, feline claws, its blood still warm.

Taking a small and keen knife from a hip sheath, Abildan sliced the doe from throat to gut. She parted skin and muscle with her hands. The ribcage broke easily, and Abildan removed it, methodically, one snap at a time like the young bones were no tougher than dry twigs. She then reached into the chest cavity. With care, she cut out the doe's heart. The organ smelled healthy and stout.

The Wyrd taught their assassins the benefits of blood magic. Not much, not enough to make the feliwyrd proficient magickers, but sufficiently to quicken already fast reflexes and heighten already honed senses. Blood magic altered the perceptions of the feliwyrd; it could show them the hidden corners of the world, reveal secret paths.

Abildan bit into the heart.

There was no fat, only muscle, and it was tough to chew. She took a second bite, a third and fourth, until the heart was devoured. She closed her eyes, whispering secret words that had been taught to her by the Wyrd.

The forest changed. Branch, root and leaf began sighing upon Abildan's senses. The hidden energy of the Great Forest whispered to her. She stood, revelling in the magic that now fuelled her body. Yellow eyes became black as night.

Stepping over the doe's corpse, Abildan approached the wall of Uljah. She growled another, single word of her masters, this one a simple command. As if cowering to the sorcery of the Wyrd, the dense foliage shivered and parted to reveal a shadowy tunnel that stretched into unknown woodlands beyond.

Pleased, Abildan stared into the gloom.

Once she entered the tunnel, her presence would be detected by the lines of power that criss-crossed the lands of Uljah. They would warn the Ulyyn of an intruder. Warriors would come for the feliwyrd. The magic of Uljah would command the forest itself to rise and attack her. But the Ulyyn knew nothing of Abildan's mission, of why the Wyrd had sent her. A game was about to begin, a game of time, a duel of the quickest, and Abildan had until the power of blood magic wore off to make the first strike.

Relishing the challenge before her, her mind and body alive with eldritch energy, the feliwyrd sprang forward and bolted down the tunnel.

Of course there was a guardian protecting the lush glade on the other side: a dryad, young and agile with long vines rising behind it, twisting and venomous. Abildan drew her curved sabre as she ran. She barely broke her stride as she cut the vines from the dryad's back and slit its throat. With a scream like moaning wind, the dryad fell and thrashed on the mossy floor. Its death throes sounded the final alarm that would announce Abildan's arrival.

She sped on, climbing the steep embankment and sprinted into the trees.

The race had begun.

The tracking instinct of the feliwyrd was legendary, but Abildan had no need of this skill now. From the visions of the oracwyrd, the way to a specific location had been implanted into her head. A sixth sense now steered her towards exactly where her quarry would be, and when.

It had been the name 'Amyya' which surfaced from the future-dreams of the oracwyrd this time. The name belonged to an Ulyyn girl, not yet old enough to have lost her innocence, but destined, at some point in her life, to hinder the machinations of the Wyrd. When considering that Amyya was a princess of the Ulyyn, some would reason that attempting her assassination was nothing short of suicide - and so it was. But assassinate her Abildan would, without question or thought of living to see Mya-Siad again.

Abildan's way was easy at first, unhindered, as she ducked beneath branches, vaulted thick roots, and followed paths that were soft underfoot. Uljah thrived with the colours and scents of summer; its land seemed somehow superior to the rest of the Great Forest, as though all unsightly growth and dullness had been swept away.

Not until Abildan stopped to drink from a stream did she encounter the next stage of the Ulyyn's resistance. The stream was narrow, its water cool and clear. While Abildan drank from cupped hands, she sensed a slight alteration in the breeze, as though the wind itself had held its breath and then sighed.

She rolled to one side, springing to her feet, sabre in hand.

Healthy leaves were falling from the trees as though dying in autumn. They did not reach the ground, however, but swirled and danced in the air, spiralling and pressing together until they formed the shape of a four-armed forest demon. With a sound like wind rushing through the trees, it bounded towards the feliwyrd.

Abildan spun and slashed the sabre across demon's midriff. The blade passed effortlessly through the leaves of its body, resealing in the sabre's wake, causing no damage whatsoever. Surprised and wrong-footed, Abildan stumbled and discovered that the demon's punch was far more substantial than its body.

A massive, stone-hard fist struck Abildan in the stomach. Her heightened reflexes allowed her to relax and absorb much of the blow, but the demon was fast and didn't let up. Blow after blow came at Abildan. She dodged and weaved with preternatural speed, barely managing to avoid the four quick fists that struck at her. When she at last gained room for a counterstrike, she slashed the demon's face, but it exploded into a storm of leaves that whipped around the feliwyrd, stinging and crushing.

The storm's grip tightened, squeezing the air from Abildan's lungs, and she dropped the sabre. Her cry of pain struggled to pass from a strangled throat. With her last breath, or so it seemed, she managed to bark a dark word of the Wyrd, calling for aid from the blood magic within her.

With a great sucking sound, the storm of leaves was drawn up into the air as though caught in a whirlwind. Like the angriest of thunder clouds, the mass hung above Abildan, droning. She drew breath and barked a second word of blood magic.

Every leaf burst into quick, white fire.

Ash drifted like snow and settled upon the forest floor.

Breathing hard, Abildan snatched up her sabre, cursing herself. Her reserve of blood magic was little enough for the task at hand. There was none spare for getting blindsided like a novice. No more time for mistakes, no more stopping until she found Princess Amyya.

She cocked her ear.

In the distance, the baying of a wolf pack filtered through the forest, coming closer. Just as the Wyrd had sent their pet to Uljah, so the Ulyyn had unleashed theirs on her.

Abildan sheathed her sabre and resumed the hunt.

The way was not as smooth as before. As she headed deeper into the forest, Abildan could feel the trees pressing in on her, as though the magic of Uljah were a thousand eyes observing her progress, tracking her every step. At least Princess Amyya was not at the heart of Uljah, where the Ulyyn dwelt in an impenetrable fortress of monstrously sized trees.

There was a tradition in these lands, a rite of passage that all nobility had to undertake in their youth. To survive alone in the wild forest of Uljah, to learn and understand the lore of its magic until it became embedded into the soul, was the only way to prove oneself worthy to a race who predated most others on Earth. Even now, Princess Amyya was taking her rite of passage, proving her worthiness to be the Queen of Uljah. And she was doing so all alone, far from the protection of her people.

The oracwyrd saw everything.

Eldritch energy burning rich in her veins, Abildan pushed herself hard, fast, to stay one step ahead of the forest's defences.

By now, the baying of the wolf pack had grown close, closer all the time. Abildan reasoned that the Ulyyn had given their dogs unnatural speed that outmatched her own. Her time was getting shorter by the heartbeat, and if she did not reach her prey soon, the teeth of the wolves would be snapping at her heels.

The forest stirred and grew thick, corralling Abildan into a narrow track where the trees loomed and their branches reached out like clawed fingers. She didn't slow and drew her sabre as she detected lines of magic growing in radiance just beneath the surface of the path, warm against the soles of her feet.

Just ahead, the first root shot from the ground, coiling like a tentacle, striking for the feliwyrd. Abildan's sabre sliced through it effortlessly, and she left it writhing on the forest floor in her wake. Another shot from the ground, and then another, until it seemed the entire length of the track was alive with the limbs of a great sea beast.

Abildan dodged and slashed her way down the maze of tentacles, ignoring the stabs and cuts she received along the way. The last of the blood magic fuelled her reactions, raised her reflexes to new heights, and she was too fast for the vicious roots. Up ahead, the track's end came into sight, and Abildan bared her teeth, fighting her way towards it.

She broke from the end of the track and emerged to where the forest parted to reveal a lush valley below her.

A scream pierced the air.

Abildan observed from the ridgeline.

On the valley floor a strange scenario played out, which the feliwyrd had not anticipated. She recognised the small figure of Amyya instantly - she had been carrying the image of her face in her mind from Mya-Siad. The princess was engaged in combat against one of Uljah's giant guardians.

A dryad attacked Amyya. Big and strong, far older than the one Abildan had slaughtered in the glade. Its limbs and body were thick and cumbersome, but its movements were powerful and surprisingly quick. Amyya darted and weaved, rolled and jumped, easily avoiding the dryad's poisonous vines and smashing fists. She was skilled and taking good stock of herself, but it was evident that she was tiring. The dryad gave no respite in which she might flee.

In the strange language of the Ulyyn, Amyya called and grunted with orders, but her efforts to temper the furious magic that compelled the dryad were in vain. It was trying its hardest to kill the princess, but this was not part of Amyya's rite of passage. Something was wrong with the creature. Abildan could sense its confusion and anger from up on the ridge. The dryad was rogue, beset by madness, and this was a fight Amyya could not win.

A cruel smile curved Abildan's lips.

Perhaps her mission would be easier than she thought. She wondered, for a moment, if there would be no need to spill blood herself. Could she simply watch the dryad do her work for her; and then, after enjoying the sport, slip away into the forest and head home to Mya-Siad?

No.

The call of the wolves was but moments away in the forest behind her. And now, high in the sky, the shapes of giant hawks were silhouetted against the sun, as were the Ulyyn warriors riding on their backs. If Amyya could keep up her fight for but a short while longer, then her people would reach her in time to save her from the insane dryad.

The irony was not lost on the feliwyrd: had she not come to Uljah, the Ulyyn would not have been drawn to her presence, and Abildan would not have led them to the plight of their princess.

Her blood magic all but depleted, Abildan accepted the inevitable. She unbuckled her sabre from her back and let it slip to the ground, scabbard and all. Sharp nails slid from her fingertips. Fighting to the death with tooth and claw alone, she would see the orders of the Wyrd obeyed. Her sacrifice, her life, willingly given for a future Earth ruled by Mya-Siad.

Driven by yowl of pride, Abildan sprinted down the slope into the valley.

She glanced up and saw the bows and spears in the hands of the Ulyyn warriors riding the great hawks. They were close, but not close enough. Halfway down the slope, Abildan risked a glance back, seeing the wolf pack burst from the tree line and stream down after her. Their barks and howls meant nothing to the feliwyrd.

Ahead, Princess Amyya tired in the battle against the dryad. She too had noticed the arrival of her people, and the notion of rescue should have given her extra courage and strength for the fight. But her attention was then caught by the feliwyrd bearing down on her, chased by the feral pack. In that moment's distraction, the dryad's vine whipped out and its poisonous sting lashed across Amyya's face.

She fell to the ground and lay still. The dryad, not content that its poison was now coursing through its prey's veins, raised both its huge fists. But before it beat down on the small and prone body, it too noticed the feliwyrd. Facing the new threat, it gave an eerie bellow of challenge.

Maddeningly, the dryad blocked Abildan's path to the princess, and the only way to her was through it. With the wolves snapping not far behind, the claws of giant hawks descending from the sky, Abildan met the creature head on.

She dodged the first vine as it lashed forth, ducked under the second, and then rolled to one side, avoiding the fist that smashed the earth beside her. Springing to her feet, Abildan leapt and gouged the dryad's eyes from their sockets, before vaulted onto its back. Blind, the dryad roared and tried to reach over its shoulder to grab its attacker. Abildan avoided the attempt. Her claws cut the vines from its back, and they fell limp to the valley floor. Revelling in the beast's screams of torture, Abildan bit into its neck.

The dryad's cries were desperate now, but no matter how it twisted and turned and thrashed, it could not dislodge the feliwyrd from its back. Abildan bit harder and deeper, down through bark-like skin until the bitter taste of sap-like blood flooded her mouth. Her teeth tore away chunks of woody flesh, the fur of her face matted with amber blood, claws stabbed into her adversary's throat. The dryad dropped to its knees, moaning, and then fell facedown, dead.

With the wolves almost upon her, Abildan wasted pounced for the immobile form of Princess Amyya.

That was when the first arrow struck her in the back.

The second thudded into her shoulder.

Abildan spun around and dropped to her knees just as the wolf pack crashed into her and bowled her over. The arrows were poison-tipped. The venom paralysed her movements and darkened her vision.

She was vaguely aware of the wolves snarling, tugging at her clothes with their sharp teeth. She heard the whoosh of wings and the thump of giant hawks landing in the valley. The strange clicks and grunts of the Ulyyn language sounded urgently around her. And as the world turned to starless night, Abildan knew that Princess Amyya would survive, and she had failed Mya-Siad.

Thirteen
Darkness

By the time Abildan finished her tale, evening had slipped into night. Mist crept through the forest and fires burned brightly in the Boskan camp.

Abildan fell silent, her fur-covered face turned to the sky and lost to the past. The four knights watched the feliwyrd, waiting for her to reveal more. But she evidently felt no inclination to say anything further.

Vladisal allowed the silence to grow for a moment longer, before saying, "The Wyrd sent you to Uljah to assassinate a princess, but the Ulyyn let you live?"

"Yes." Abildan's voice was barely above a whisper.

Luca shook her head. "Not very likely."

"I'll say," Dief added.

"Not only did they let you live, but also rewarded you with a talisman of friendship?" Üban barked a single, derisive laugh.

Her face unreadable, Abildan scanned the camp behind the four knights, and all hint of mockery left her manner.

"I warned you that the Ulyyn were a hard race to understand," she said, pointedly to Vladisal. "Regardless of my mission, had I not come to the Great Forest then Princess Amyya would have died at the hands of the mad dryad. However inadvertently, I saved her life, and the Ulyyn regard a life-debt as a sacred thing. The leaf talisman honours their debt to me. A strange scenario, yes, but that is the bare truth of it."

Abildan seemed genuine, but old Üban was not to be convinced.

"You and I have very different understandings of the truth, feliwyrd."

"You think me a liar, and your convictions are, perhaps, justified to a

61

degree." Abildan's tone was detached, her eyes still scanned the camp. "No one was more surprised than I that the Ulyyn spared my life."

"And so did Mya-Siad," Luca pointed out. "The Wyrd are famed for many things, but leniency in the face of failure is not among them."

"This tale grows harder to believe by the second," Üban growled.

Dief made to say something, but coughed instead, spitting on the ground as though ridding her mouth of a foul taste.

"Ladies, please." Abildan sighed. "I am feliwyrd. My lot is to serve, not to question, not to understand. I can only presume that my masters foresaw a day when the life-debt owed to me by the Ulyyn would be useful to their plans. Perhaps Mya-Siad foresaw the problem of Dun-Wyrd."

"Oh, this is rich," Üban said. She gave a sour chuckle. "The Bone Shakers have sent their monster here because it benefits their dreams of enslaving Earth? Is that it?"

"What else did you expect, Sir Üban?" There was no retort in Abildan's reply. "The future dreams of the oracwyrd see many things, which only the Wyrd can decipher. Perhaps Dun-Wyrd's death has to happen. Perhaps the parts played by Elander and the Knights of Boska were also foreseen. Was my failure to kill the princess planned all along? Was gaining a favour from the Ulyyn the real goal of mission? The road to Mya-Siad's future could take centuries to walk, and no moment of that journey is inconsequential."

The feliwyrd frowned, seemed troubled. "But then again, it is possible that my failure reaped unexpected benefits. Dun-Wyrd might have been sentenced to death for simple treachery. Elander's abduction, our alliance, the Ulyyn, could all be coincidence. Only the Wyrd know if it is luck or fate that drives us."

Vladisal wondered if Abildan, at long last, was offering a degree of sincerity to the Knights of Boska. It seemed to be the case, but it was so hard to tell.

"What and why make no difference," Üban said, her voice low. "Whether Redheart can use the talisman to bring the Ulyyn to us or not, our mission does not change. I will suffer no more of dreams and futures."

"Spoken like a true pragmatist," Abildan said, without mockery.

"No, wait." Luca's scepticism remained. "I'm still curious even if you are not, Üban. I do not wish to sound quarrelsome, Abildan, but I think you know more than you're saying about what Dun-Wyrd is doing in the Great Forest."

Abildan's eyes lingered on Vladisal. "If you must force me to make an educated guess, then I believe that Dun-Wyrd has turned separatist. If I am right, then the Great Forest would make a perfect location to build a new Wyrd empire in secret, far from Mya-Siad. And the Ulyyn would make powerful allies."

"Allies?" Üban almost laughed. "We have all heard what Luca has said, and the Ulyyn would never ally themselves with a Bone Shaker."

"Not through choice," Abildan said. "But Dun-Wyrd could bend them to her will. In time. Her first step towards building a new empire will be to create her very own oracwyrd."

"A future-dreamer…" Luca's scepticism grew. She shook her head at Vladisal and Üban. "It takes decades of torturous procedure to create an oracwyrd-"

"You wished to know what I believed, and now I am telling you!" Abildan snapped, exasperated. "Never underestimate how intelligent and resourceful Dun-Wyrd is. Her tree-demons have already shown you how well she can manipulate the magic of the Great Forest, and the power of that magic increases tenfold in the lands of Uljah."

Abildan impatience shone through. She glared at each knight in turn. "If Dun-Wyrd wishes to corrupt and bend the Ulyyn to her rule, then she must learn how to turn Uljah's magic against its people. And she will decipher how to do exactly that through the dreams of a future-seer. She will create a new kind of oracwyrd, and it will not take her decades! She will merge an Ulyyn, one already touched by the magic of Uljah, with a human child who was born with a particular magical gift."

A sudden, hard silence followed Abildan's words.

Vladisal felt her insides turn to ice and a name tumbled from her lips. "Elander."

Old Üban, so rational yet so superstitious, snorted a laugh. "What nonsense is this? Elander has many charms, but magic is not one of them."

Abildan raised an eyebrow. "Perhaps it is not my place to say."

Vladisal couldn't hold the feliwyrd's cold, yellow stare. She looked to the ground, unwilling to meet the frowns of Luca and Üban.

"Vlad?" said Dief.

"What is it, lass?" Üban prompted.

Vladisal took a deep breath. "My friends, I would have taken you into my confidence earlier, but I was sworn to secrecy. What I'm about to tell you must not extend to the women."

Instinctively, Luca, Üban and Dief gave their word to their captain.

Vladisal rubbed the back of her head. "This past year, Elander has changed. He has dreams. He…"

She trailed off and Abildan filled the silence.

"Elander has the Sight," she said bluntly. "He sees visions of the future."

Üban opened her mouth to speak but said nothing.

Luca gave the feliwyrd an appraising look before turning to her captain. "Is this true, Vlad?"

"Yes," Vladisal said a little angrily. "I know it, and so does his mother. Let us keep level heads, my friends. This matter is not one for open discussion."

But Dief did not care to extend any rationality to the conversation. "Elander is a witch?"

"Put your superstitions aside," said Abildan. "As Üban said, your mission has not changed."

Üban ignored the feliwyrd. "Can he be cured of this curse?"

Abildan hissed with irritation. "You wanted answers and now you have them."

Üban made to argue further, but Abildan stopped her with a raised hand and an almost pleading expression.

"The forest city of Uljah is steeped in old magic, and Dun-Wyrd will learn how to use it. Merged with the spirit of an Ulyyn, Elander's gift of Sight will be increased exponentially. He will see far into many secrets, and Dun-Wyrd will discover the future she craves."

The mist in the forest was growing thicker, and it swirled as a breeze rustled through the trees. Vladisal shivered. Üban and Luca shared a look. Abildan stepped forward, paused beside Dief, seemed to sniff her before turning her nose to the air to sniff some more.

"Think of me what you will," the feliwyrd said, stepping past the knights and casting a shrewd gaze over the camp. "But without the leaf talisman the Ulyyn will never be tempted out of their realm. They will not know of Dun-Wyrd's presence, they will not see her coming, and she will be free to turn the magic of Uljah against them. If Redheart is not successful, then only we few stand in Dun-Wyrd's way."

Abildan turned to face the knights, a laconic grin spreading across her face. "You should have listened to me. I told you to burn your dead."

Shouts came from the camp. Vladisal saw the company rushing about. A knight called for her captain.

"Vladisal! The dead are rising!"

Fourteen
Captive Audience

Redheart suspected that night had fallen, but it was impossible to tell for sure.

She had been moved from the cage to a detention cell inside one of the behemoth trees that grew in the city of Uljah. The only source of light came from soft torch flames flickering through a little barred window on the locked and sturdy door. She saw and heard no one, and could do nothing but wait, sitting on the mossy floor, surrounded by dancing shadows.

She prayed to the Mother for patience and guidance. She prayed for Vladisal and the Knights of Boska. She prayed for Elander.

Redheart had been thinking about the angry Ulyyn woman. Her grasp of human language had been awkward at best – though, oddly, she had no trouble understanding her captive. She hadn't let Redheart speak about anything other than Abildan, though Redheart had tried. The Ulyyn had a burning, furious obsession with the feliwyrd. Redheart had tried her best to understand and answer question after question, but she simply didn't know where Abildan was in the Great Forest, or her friends. And that had only served to increase the Ulyyn's fury.

Finally, with exasperation, she had ordered the guards to take her captive to the cell, and that had been when Redheart had discovered something astonishing about this Ulyyn woman. Her name was Amyya, and she was Queen of Uljah.

Redheart rubbed her face. Her wound had scabbed over, and it itched maddeningly. Hunger gripped her stomach in nauseating pangs.

The smooth wooden walls of the cell were close, and the ceiling was low. Redheart tried to ignore a sense of claustrophobia and, not for the first time, was overwhelmed by frustration. She wondered how her friends were faring. Did they recognise the depth of treachery that hid in their midst?

It seemed unbelievable that Abildan, a servant of the Wyrd, had had previous dealings with the queen of such a mythical race as the Ulyyn. But Redheart had gleaned enough from Amyya's bitter interrogation to understand that it was true. The feliwyrd had come to Uljah before. But it was clear now that the leaf talisman was no token of friendship. It served only as some insult to the Ulyyn of which Redheart herself was the unwitting culprit. Did Abildan know this would happen? Was this her plan all along?

Redheart checked an impulse to beat down the cell door with her bare hands. She was a Knight of Boska, not some animal to be kept in a cage. Yet Queen Amyya had not cared about Elander's plight; she would not be warned of the peril that had come to the Great Forest. She cared for nothing but Abildan and whatever tricks the feliwyrd was evidently playing on them all.

Despair, it seemed, was but moments away from engulfing Redheart. On her knees, eyes squeezed shut, hands clasped before her, she prayed once again to the Mother. And within her prayers, like a spark of light in the shadows, she found the face of her dearest friend Vladisal, and with it a slither of hope to which she could cling: Redheart was still alive. The day was not lost yet.

A noise came from outside.

The cell door unlocked.

Redheart got to her feet, head mere inches from the ceiling, and backed up against the far wall as the door opened.

Torchlight spilled into the cell, followed by two Ulyyn guards, armoured and wielding spears. They stood either side of the door, their weapons pointed at the prisoner. Queen Amyya stepped inside. Redheart dropped to one knee and bowed to the Ulyyn monarch.

With a gesture from her hand, Amyya bade her rise.

She was dressed as she was earlier, in robes that appeared to be made from material of the forest. But there was no anger on her small, green-tinged face. She expressed a degree of sympathy. She offered Redheart a wooden bowl, filled with steaming food. Redheart's stomach growled when she took, but she did not eat.

Amyya spoke in her own language, giving an order that the guards were hesitant to follow at first. She spoke again, her clicks and grunts harsher this time. The guards looked at each other, bowed to their monarch, and then left the cell, leaving the door open.

Amyya pointed to the bowl of food. "Eat," she said.

It was some kind of thick broth, smelling of the forest. Redheart lifted the bowl to her lips and ate hungrily. It tasted earthy. Wholesome. Filling.

Queen Amyya waited until she had finished, and then offered Redheart a small object which she held out between thumb and forefinger. Redheart wiped her mouth, placed the empty bowl on the floor, and accepted a stone of yellow glass, small like those set into rings. Confused, she gave Amyya a questioning look. By way of explanation, Amyya pulled a similar stone from her ear, which she then pushed back into place, gesturing for Redheart to do the same. Tentatively, the knight pushed the stone into her ear.

Amyya spoke. Her language clicked and grunted. The stone vibrated inside Redheart's ear, and she understood what the queen was saying.

"You Boskans are known to the Spirits of the Forest. They tell me you are women of honour."

Her voice carried a soft lilt that didn't match the movements of her mouth or the sounds it made. Redheart didn't know what manner of magic made her understand this woman, but she had to resist the urge to pluck the stone from her ear and throw it far from her.

Amyya, obviously impatient with the Boskan knight's trepidation, repeated her question a little more forcefully. "You are women of honour, yes?"

"We... We are," Redheart said.

"Yet you would ally yourself with an abomination such as the feliwyrd. This is strange."

Unnerved to have the Ulyyn's voice in her head, Redheart nodded. "It is a complicated story, Highness."

"You said many things to me earlier, things that I was too angry to acknowledge. You tried to tell me of a lost boy?"

"Yes, the son of my duchess – his name is Elander."

Amyya began to pace in front of the open doorway, her hands clasped before her. Redheart was struck by how small and delicate the Queen of Uljah was. She barely stood as tall as Redheart's chest, and her thoughtful expression seemed to belong to the face of a child.

She said, "When I was a princess, I too was lost. And I would have died had Abildan not saved me."

Redheart was surprised to say the least. "Abildan saved your life?"

This situation grew stranger by the moment. "I thought she was your enemy."

"Yes, she is always that." Amyya stopped pacing and gave Redheart a small smile. "As you say, the story is complicated. You told me earlier that a great evil has come to these lands, but it was not Abildan that you spoke of, was it?"

"No." Redheart felt a surge of hope. "A Wyrd of Mya-Siad has come to the Great Forest."

Amyya's smile disappeared. She stared at Redheart for a long moment, deliberating.

"Many years ago the Wyrd tried to kill me, but Abildan saved my life instead. By accident. The feliwyrd has let you believe that the leaf talisman is a token of friendship. It is not. There is no word in your language for the talisman's Ulyyn name, but you must think of it as a double-edged blade."

"Highness, the Wyrd-"

Amyya cut Redheart off with a raised hand. Her tawny eyes drifted up into memory. "The Spirits of the Forest teach us that to place one's own life in mortal danger for the preservation of another's is the greatest honour one can bestow. We revere this teaching, even for an abomination like a feliwyrd. It is a... saintly act, you would say?" She waited for Redheart to give an uncertain nod. "The leaf talisman was given to Abildan to acknowledge the debt of life which I owe her. In return, she may ask one favour of the Ulyyn."

Again, Redheart tried to interject. Again, Amyya silenced her.

"To claim her debt, Abildan must return to the Ulyyn. She may ask her favour, and it will be granted. However, she must also stand trial for her crimes. This is the way of Uljah. Abildan saved me but intended to kill me, and the Spirits of the Forest will not pardon that. The feliwyrd is marked as a hero and enemy both. The talisman represents her reward and execution, and hers alone. The debt is not yours to claim, Sir Redheart."

Redheart's mouth opened, but no words followed.

"The Elders of Uljah are gathered and waiting," Amyya said. "I will take you to them now. They will hear your story and decide what to do with you."

With a cold swell of despair, Redheart dropped to her knees and bowed her head. "Queen Amyya," she begged. "I am not your enemy. I do not know why Dun-Wyrd had come to the Great Forest, but the Bone Shaker has abducted Elander. He is just a child!"

Amyya approached Redheart, lifting her face to meet her own with a small and delicate hand. She expressed sadness. "I know your heart is true, woman of Boska, and I share your pain." Her voice trembled slightly. "A prince of Uljah is missing like your Elander. His name is Kyjah. He is my son."

Redheart got to her feet. "Abducted? By Dun-Wyrd?"

"Perhaps." Amyya composed herself. "When the Spirits of the Forest last visited my dreams, they warned me that a stranger would come to Uljah. They told me that my son's fate would be tied to her. For this reason, I will do all I can to help you when you stand before the Elders."

Without further word, Amyya left the cell. Redheart stared at the empty doorway until the Ulyyn guards entered. The points of their spears urged her out. More confused and desperate than ever, Redheart followed the queen.

Fifteen
The Risen

Vladisal stood at the head of the company. Üban, Luca and Dief formed a line behind her. Behind them, thirteen knights and five archers awaited orders from their captain, silent and still. Only the sound of crackling campfires disturbed the night.

Vladisal could feel the tension in the air, the fear, the horrified expression of every woman as they watched the corpses of Sir Theodora and Sir Brennik claw free of their graves.

Clumsily, the dead knights rose. Dirt and leaves clung to their armour. Their faces were ashen, slack, devoid of emotion, betraying the first signs of rot. Eyes closed as though asleep, Theodora and Brennik swayed gently on their feet.

"What madness is this?" Üban growled, but the old knight already knew the answer, as did Vladisal and every woman present.

"Dun-Wyrd does so like to play her games," said Abildan. The feliwyrd emerged through the crowd and stood alongside Vladisal. She studied the ghouls. "Even the slightest sting from a tree-demon will reduce a woman to this."

Perhaps reacting to the sound of Abildan's voice, the dead knights opened their eyes to reveal ghostly blue lights. Sir Brennik balled her hands into fists and relaxed them again, as though remembering the strength of life. Sir Theodora opened her mouth and gave a low, pained groan.

A murmur of worry rippled through the company, coupled by the clank of armour as several knights stepped back. Vladisal held her ground - as did Üban, Luca and Dief. Even when Theodora and Brennik choked on the roots which slithered from their mouths, tasting the air like the tongues if snakes, they did not move.

"Fire would have rid their bodies of Dun-Wyrd's magic," Abildan said, and she drew the sabre from her back. "But removing their heads will work just as well now." She looked at Vladisal and shrugged. "Shall I?"

"Stay your blade, Abildan," Vladisal said. "This duty is not yours to perform."

She drew her sword with a sharp ring of steel. Vladisal's loathing and despair disappeared, falling flat to the dejection of utmost misery. No one said a word, no one tried to stop her, as she raised her sword and stepped towards her reanimated knights.

"Here is the peace that Dun-Wyrd would steal from you," she said in a strong, clear voice. Her blade took the head of Sir Brennik. "May the Mother God welcome your souls into heaven," and Sir Theodora joined her sister knight back in the ground, headless and at rest.

In the following silence, not even Abildan had a caustic remark to utter.

Vladisal felt Üban's hand on her shoulder.

"Had to be done, Vlad. No shame in your actions."

"This is not ended yet," Vladisal replied darkly, her voice stone. "Dun-Wyrd's tree-demons could be upon us any moment."

She turned from the graves to address the company. In the flickering light, fear and hopelessness shrouded each of their faces. Vladisal's misery became wrath.

"Light more fires!" Her order came as a loud, harsh bark. "Set a perimeter! Watch the trees! If the Bone Shaker thinks she can so easily frighten us, then she knows nothing of Boskan women!"

Inspired to action, the knights set about their captain's orders with haste and proficiency.

Vladisal turned to her three friends. "Luca, Dief, organise the women. Üban, position the archers."

Luca and Dief strode off, shouting more orders. Before Üban followed them, she clapped Vladisal on the shoulder. "Welcome back, my captain."

Abildan remained. Her thin lips were twisted into a half smile.

"Something amuses you?" Vladisal said levelly.

"A rousing speech, but your women waste their time." Abildan lifted an eyebrow. "Dun-Wyrd has no need to send her army here tonight. Her monsters are already hiding in your camp."

A cry broke out among the milling knights, followed by several more. A commotion began. Üban called for her captain, and Vladisal rushed over.

The women had formed a circle around two knights. Sir Mervya was on her knees, holding the side of her neck. Blood leaked from between her fingers, and there was a look of shock in her eyes as she gazed up at Sir Finn.

Finn backed away from her sister knight, disgust and confusion decorating her face. There was blood around her mouth. She gagged and spat a fleshy mass onto the ground.

"What's the meaning of this?" Vladisal demanded.

"She… she bit me," Sir Mervya said, a trembling finger pointed at Finn. "Tore a chunk out of me."

Vladisal made to approach Finn, but the knight drew her sword, pointing it at her captain. "Stay back!" she shouted.

It was a warning, not a threat.

"Finn?" Vladisal said.

"It hurts," Finn sobbed. "It's like fire in my veins."

Groaning in pain, she dropped the sword and doubled over, vomiting blood onto the ground. She then straightened, abruptly, arching her back, opening her mouth wide. And then, with all the fury of the hells, Finn screamed at the night sky.

Sir Mervya scrambled away. The knights stepped back, widening the circle around Finn, some of them drawing weapons. When Finn's scream died, her head hung slack, as though she slept while standing.

A stunned stillness followed. Vladisal looked to where Üban stood between Luca and Dief behind Finn. The old knight stared back at Vladisal, teeth clenched.

Sir Finn looked up. Blue light shone from her eyes. More weapons were drawn. A line of blood ran from Finn's mouth and down her breastplate, but she did not groan. No roots snaked from her mouth.

She turned full circle, scrutinising the band of knights surrounding her with a smile that was cold and cruel. She faced Vladisal and the light of her eyes flared.

"Sir Vladisal." Finn's chuckle was low and whispery. "A pleasure, I'm sure."

Her voice was thin and dry, and most certainly not belonging to Finn. Rage clawed up Vladisal's throat; she knew who was addressing her.

"What do you want?"

"Oh, I think it's high time we had a talk, don't you?"

"You and I have nothing to discuss, Dun-Wyrd."

At the mention of that name, any woman who had not yet bared arms did so keenly.

"Are you really so sure?" Dun-Wyrd said through Finn's corpse. "It seems that we have much in common these days."

"Be gone, Bone Shaker," Vladisal spat. "Leave my woman's spirit in peace. We will meet soon enough, but never on your terms."

Finn considered that. "For all your brave words, Sir Knight, you must realise that you are only leading a band of frightened girls lost in the woods."

"You do not frighten me!" Vladisal snarled.

"Nor I," Üban bellowed.

"Or any woman here," Luca added.

Dief hefted her hammer but said nothing.

The rest of the knights found courage in these declarations. Vladisal could read it in their body language.

Finn's corpse gave a cursory glance over her shoulder. "Nonetheless, I will extend a onetime offer to you and your brave women. Leave the Great Forest, tonight, and I will hinder you no more. Stay, and you will join my army."

Vladisal pointed at the Bone Shaker with her sword. The blade was stained with the blood of Theodora and Brennik. "We will leave after you return Elander to us."

"Ah, yes - the boy. Would it make any difference to your decision if I told you that he was already dead?"

Vladisal felt cold and her voice shook. "If that is true, then I will not leave the Great Forest until I have your head in a bag."

"Courageously spoken, Sir Knight, but I don't take kindly to threats." The blue light of Sir Finn's dead eyes pulsed. "Your pride will condemn every woman here."

"Fear us, Bone Shaker!" Vladisal shouted. Her tone was iron. "We know what you plan, and we know how to stop you."

Dun-Wyrd clasped her hands together and laughed with genuine humour. "You believe you can stop me? Why? Because an assassin of Mya-Siad has joined your cause?" Sir Finn's corpse turned in a circle again, searching the ranks of knights. "Where is the feliwyrd? I know she is among you, but I do not see her now." She sighed at Vladisal. "Abildan is a liar, a trickster. She is here to serve me, not you."

"Then by all means," Vladisal said with low tones, "call her to your side."

"You fool," Dun-Wyrd hissed. "Never forget that the feliwyrd are bred to serve the Wyrd. It is in Abildan's blood-"

Sir Finn's head snapped back. Dun-Wyrd's voice cried out in pain and surprise. The corpse sank to its knees. The cry faded, as did the light in Finn's eyes. The flight of a crossbow bolt protruded from her forehead.

Abildan walked into the circle. She hooked her single-handed crossbow onto her belt and strode up to the dead knight. With a foot, she pushed Finn onto her back, then turned to Vladisal.

"Elander is still alive," she said, her feline features demonic in the firelight. "Be assured of that."

Around Abildan, the knights seemed to close in menacingly. The way the feliwyrd had dealt with their sister had turned fear to anger.

Misreading the source of their chagrin, Abildan said, "Tell your women not to be fooled. I am here to kill Dun-Wyrd, not serve her. Tell them now, Sir Vladisal."

Vladisal's eyes lingered on her fallen knight "You do not order me, Abildan." Her lip curled. "Sir Finn was a woman of Boska, and it was not your place to give her spirit mercy."

"Mercy?" Abildan cast her yellow gaze around the company. "Understand me," she said to all, "Dun-Wyrd's magic is carried by her army. It is a disease nourished by blood. It is spread by spores that hide in the mouth-roots of every tree-demon. They can pass infection by causing the smallest would. Any woman here stung by a tree-demon will share Sir Finn's fate."

Abildan looked at Sir Mervya who still knelt, clutching her neck wound, her face panicked. "And when your eyes glow with the blue light of the damned, I will not hesitate to give you my mercy."

"How dare you." It was Üban. The old knight confronted Abildan, sword in hand. "You and Dun-Wyrd do not decide our fate."

"No," Abildan said heatedly. "That is the duty of your cursed Mother God."

Üban gave a cry of rage and raised her sword.

"Üban!" Vladisal shouted.

Too late. Üban prepared to strike down, but the feliwyrd was far quicker than the aging warrior. While the sword remained in the air, Abildan drew her sabre and touched its keen blade to Üban's throat.

"Could you do it, old woman?" Abildan hissed. "Could you give one of your dearest friends peace from the horrors of Dun-Wyrd's magic?"

Üban grunted, frozen with her sword raised above her head.

Stillness. Not a knight stirred. A heartbeat passed, before Luca's voice disturbed the moment.

"Where's Dief?"

The big knight was no longer beside her friends. Vladisal looked around the camp, seeing her nowhere.

"Sir Dief has fled into the forest," Abildan said. She removed the sabre from Üban's throat, and the old knight stumbled back. "She was stung during the battle last night, but told no one. This night has shown her what end that wound will bring her."

"No," said Luca. "We have to find her."

She called Dief's name, and then again more urgently.

"Let your friend go, Sir Luca," Abildan said. She addressed Vladisal and Üban. "Sir Dief has spores in her veins and she feels the calling of Dun-Wyrd's curse. I would advise letting her chose her own end while her dignity remains and she still recognises you as sisters." She slid her sabre into the sheath on her back. "And ask yourselves, who else among you is infected with the Bone-Shaker's disease."

Abildan pushed her way through the gathering of knights to the edge of the camp. No one tried to stop her. The feliwyrd's words, it seemed, had put ice in everyone's bones.

"By all means search for Dief, if that is the Boskan way, Sir Vladisal," Abildan called as she disappeared into the trees. "But know that tomorrow will bring a true test of your courage."

Vladisal realised that her hand had clenched into a fist. She didn't relax it. Luca's voice was growing in panic as she paced along the tree line, calling for Dief. The knights were staring at their captain for guidance, for reassurance, but Vladisal could not find words for them. She felt numbed, lost.

Who else indeed had been infected?

She looked at Sir Mervya, nursing her wound. Her eyes were closed and tears ran down her cheeks. The women were keeping their distance from her.

Sixteen
Judgement

With her control of the knight's dead body severed so abruptly, Dun-Wyrd cried out and held a hand to the wall to steady herself. Breath came in short, harsh gasps.

Wolves began howling.

Dun-Wyrd waited, listening as their voices ebbed into a few lonely whines that drifted through the pitch-dark corridors of the lair. She steadied her breathing and wiped beads of sweat from her bald head. A thin smile came to her gaunt face.

Sir Vladisal and her knights were brave, Dun-Wyrd had to give them that. But their stubborn pride would prove to be their undoing.

She raised the hood of her robe, feeling a chill in her fragile body and stick-thin limbs. Shivering, she left the small chamber and walked down a long corridor where not one single torch burned. Her eyes needed no light to see her lair, for magic infused every part of her and she no longer had to rely on such basic senses. She was a mighty Wyrd... though some sought to strip her of that title.

Bitter disappointment prickled Dun-Wyrd's thoughts. Her brothers and sisters back in Mya-Siad had long ago lost their way. For centuries they had studied the dreams of the oracwyrd, but still they had not cultivated a world under their rule. For generations they had been sowing the seeds of a future which they just could not bring to pass. The Wyrd had such faith in their starched and resolute methods that they had blinded themselves to their own foibles. They could not see the simpler vision that would hasten a world dominated by Mya-Siad. But Dun-Wyrd could see it; and soon she would show her brother and sister Wyrd the error of their ways.

Reaching the end of the corridor, she turned right and came to another of the lair's small chambers. She paused in the doorway to observe her prisoners. Two of them, held within cocoons of transparent, sorcerous energy. The magic gave off the dullest of grey glows, which, to normal eyes, barely illuminated the captives beyond silhouettes.

The first was the Boskan boy, Elander. He was handsome enough, Dun-Wyrd supposed, but not so regal looking now. His long, raven hair was lank and matted; his face was filthy and his clothes were tatty and stained.

When Dun-Wyrd had first abducted Elander in Mayland, he had whimpered and sobbed until it had seemed her tears would be endless. Dun-Wyrd had placed him in a catatonic state, and kept him thus now. Standing rigid and motionless within the magical cocoon, Elander's face was lax, looking for all the world to be already dead. But he would wake, soon, though he would never remember the person he had been.

The second captive was an Ulyyn boy. He was small and appeared a little younger than Elander – though it was hard to tell with this race. He wore a simple gown that almost blended with the earthy colour of his skin. A creature of the forest, his heritage rich in mysticism.

His name was Kyjah, and he was a jewel among the Ulyyn, a prince of Uljah. Dun-Wyrd had found him alone in the forest, conducting the ridiculous and archaic rite of passage that was so important to Ulyyn culture. Perhaps he thought it had been his own decision to stray beyond the borders of Uljah, curious as to what lay outside his homeland. All he had discovered was a Wyrd waiting for him. Unlike Elander, Kyjah had required no subduing.

The Ulyyn prince quite calmly sat cross-legged within his magical confinement, eyes closed in meditation, face twitching with concentration. Kyjah was searching for lines of magic that criss-crossed the Great Forest. He hoped to reach out to his people through this magic, call for help, and his naivety amused Dun-Wyrd.

Her lair was far from Uljah. There was no way Kyjah could reach his people from here. And even if he could, the Ulyyn had long ago shunned the world. They were not like the Knights of Boska; they would not step from their borders to search the Great Forest for a lost boy, even if he was their prince.

Pleased, Dun-Wyrd left her prisoners to whatever nightmares plagued their dreams, and continued down the corridor. She felt how dry and crumbling the lair had become. This place had all but outlived its

Edward Cox

usefulness, and the time had come to abandon it in favour of a new sanctuary, perhaps one in the lands of Uljah itself. A pleasing thought.

Dun-Wyrd walked through the darkness to the chamber where she kept her most cherished possession.

It was a contraption fashioned from grey stone. Plain and rough, the size and shape of an ale keg, it hovered a few feet from the ground, radiating supernatural energy. Dun-Wyrd approached it and opened the small doors set into its stone body.

Light suffused the chamber.

An orb of green magic swirled in the contraption's belly. It hummed with a discordant drone, spitting sparks of energy that buzzed like a swarm of angry bees. Dun-Wyrd had cast this spell two days ago, after she had captured Kyjah. It had been steadily growing to maturity ever since. And now, it was ready.

The Melding Arc, the contraption was called. A favourite toy of the Wyrd. For centuries they had used these devices to create their armies, merging humanoids with the spirits of… all manner of life. Dun-Wyrd had used it to create her tree-demons, and soon Vladisal and her knights would learn how the Melding Arc worked. All that the green swirling magic needed now was exposure to a natural energy source.

Dun-Wyrd sucked in a shuddery breath and stilled her anticipation.

When morning came, the rays of the sun would power the Melding Arc, and Dun-Wyrd would create a new breed of oracwyrd. The magic of the Ulyyn ran strong in Prince Kyjah's veins. Not only would his heritage enhance Elander's gift of Sight to see far into many futures, it would also reveal the ancient secrets of Uljah itself. Dun-Wyrd's new empire would spread throughout the Great Forest and beyond to dominate all Earth.

A wolf's howl echoed through the lair like the wails of a ghost.

Hands shaking, Dun-Wyrd closed the Melding Arc's doors. The light of the spell vanished. Her smile returned as more wolves added their voices to the first, and the cacophony reverberated like thunder.

With the rising of the next sun, Elander and Kyjah would be merged into a single being, the Ulyyn would bend to the way of the Wyrd, and Mya-Siad would hail Dun-Wyrd as a pioneer, the visionary who gave sight to the blind eyes of her brothers and sisters.

Seventeen
Elder Wisdom

Redheart had attended court at Mayland Castle many times over the years. She had spent more hours than she cared to count listening to bureaucrats pontificating and squabbling over trials and laws to the point of pettiness. On occasion, she and Vladisal had been given leave to administer the law in Duchess Mayland's stead; and Redheart liked to think they always did so justly. But never before had she been the sole attention of court, never once had she stood trial, and never had she dreamed to find herself at the mercy of such strange judges.

The Elders of Uljah sat upon ornate wooden thrones, arranged in a semi-circle. There were seven in all, and Redheart knelt before them. Surrounding the spectacle, hundreds of diminutive Ulyyn observed from the ascending rows of bench seats which formed the open-air theatre. Redheart kept her gaze firmly fixed upon the wooden floor, unwilling to meet the eyes of any present.

Earlier, Redheart had gained a grander view of Uljah when Amyya had brought her to the theatre on the back of a giant hawk. The great bird had soared high and fast, and Redheart had clung to the Ulyyn Queen, fearing she might fall. From the air, the fires of the city had twinkled like stars as far as Redheart could see. Uljah was vast, covering many hectares of the Great Forest, and this theatre seemed to serve as the city's focal point.

Now, on her knees beneath the moon and stars, surrounded by warm flames dancing in braziers, Redheart dared to look at the Elders.

Each of their faces were hidden in the shadows of hooded robes. They talked among themselves in voices too low for the magical glass stone in Redheart's ear to translate. Four guards were present on the theatre floor. Two were positioned on either end of the semi-circle of thrones. The other two stood a few paces behind Redheart, guarding her with spears. The host of Ulyyn citizens watched proceedings with eerie silence.

Redheart felt small and insignificant under the scrutiny of such a large audience. But she gained a little comfort from the presence of Queen Amyya, who stood beside her, patient and regal. Even on her knees, Redheart's face was almost level with hers.

Amyya smiled unconvincingly at her. "The Elders are discussing you," her voice whispered in Redheart's ear. "They are deciding if there is truth to your story." She nodded towards the thrones. "The Head Elder sits on the centre throne. She will listen to the advice of her fellows, but she alone will speak for the council."

All speech was indeed directed at the centre Elder. Redheart tried to quell the anxiety rising in her gut.

Long minutes had passed since she had given her testimony. In a shaking voice, Redheart had told the Elders of Elander's abduction, of the chase from Boska, of the unlikely alliance formed with Abildan; and, lastly, of the dreaded Wyrd of Mya-Siad who had come to the Great Forest. Amyya had translated her words in a loud, strong voice for the audience of Ulyyn, who did not have the benefit of the magical stones like the Elders. When Redheart had finished, no one had stirred. The multitude of small, forest-coloured face looked down silently at their strange visitor. And the Elders did not question Redheart's story, offered no reactions, and seemed quite content to deliberate the information among themselves.

All things considered, Redheart felt confused and frustrated. The Ulyyn were so underwhelmed by her revelations that it was as if these troubles belonged to a far and distant land.

In the enduring silence, Redheart whispered to Amyya. "You did not mention Kyjah. When you told your people my story, you said nothing of your son."

Amyya's face darkened. "The purpose of this council is not to discuss the matter of Prince Kyjah." The reply was blunt. She said no more on the matter.

Redheart eyed her curiously.

When she had addressed her people, Amyya had spoken with passion and confidence, humble but commanding. She obviously believed Redheart and understood that Dun-Wyrd's presence effected them all. Yet it had seemed as though the audience had regarded their queen with the same air which they regarded Redheart. There was a lack of respect, a lack of trust, as though Amyya's word carried little weight.

Redheart suspected that the Queen of the Ulyyn was no more than a figurehead, and the true rule of Uljah lay in the hands of the Elders. Did only they decide the outcome of this impossible to fathom council?

Her frustration growing, Redheart leaned a little closer to Amyya. "Forgive me, your highness, but your Elders do not seem concerned that a Wyrd has come to their lands. If she came to Boska, we would ride to meet her."

Amyya shook her head. "Dun-Wyrd has not stepped within our borders, Sir Redheart. She is not yet Uljah's concern."

"Not your concern? You say that your son's fate is tied with mine, with Elander's. Surely you understand that this must mean Kyjah was abducted by Dun-Wyrd, too?"

"Yes. I understand." Amyya cast her furtive gaze over the semi-circle of Elders up on the stage. She then scanned the denizens in the theatre as though suspicious, or resentful. "But you must understand that our ways are not your ways. The Elders have no interest in my son. Not anymore."

Redheart frowned. "No one has searched for him? No one cares that he is missing?"

"I care!" Amyya hissed. Angry. Hurt. "But the Elders will not listen to my pleas." Her voice dropped to barely a sigh. "Kyjah is lost forever, they say."

Tears sprang to Amyya's eyes. She wiped them away with agitated strokes. In that moment Redheart knew that her earlier suspicions were correct. The queen did not hold the reins of power in Uljah.

A loud knocking disturbed the moment.

The Head Elder banged a wooden ball against the arm of her throne. The sound carried across the theatre, echoing out into the forest of behemoth trees, clear and loud amidst the quiet of the audience.

"Woman of Boska!" The Head Elder's voice came from the depths of her hood, clicks and grunts that vibrated the stone in Redheart's ear, becoming intelligible words in her mind. "You have come to us as an unwelcome visitor, but the Spirits of the Forest respect that you came in peace and your need is great. We judge you a fool but no liar."

The audience stirred for the first time, and a score of hushed voices filled Redheart's mind in a mash of incoherent whispers.

"However," the Elder continued. "The problems of your world do not belong to the Ulyyn. Therefore, we will allow you to leave our lands, and may you never return."

This time the hushed voices were louder, as if the entire crowd were now on the verge of protesting. Redheart looked to Amyya, confused.

"The Elders are permitting you to live," she was clearly surprised by this decision, and disappointed by the crowd's growing discontent. "The citizens think you are untrustworthy, a lair, and they expected your execution."

"Execution?" Redheart was appalled, panicked. She gritted her teeth. "They cannot send me away. They have to help! My friends, your son, will die!"

Amyya's steely gaze remained on her people.

The Head Elder banged the wooden ball. The crowd audience fell silent once again.

"The Elders speak for the Spirits of the Forest," she said. "All will heed our word. Woman of Boska, we will escort you to our borders and bid you well in your quest."

The ball banged once more with finality, signalling the end of the council. Amyya faced the night sky, eyes closed, a tear on her cheek.

Desperation flamed Redheart's soul. "No!" she shouted.

The citizens erupted with jeers of outrage. The magical stone translated enough for Redheart to understand that it was an insult to question the word of the Elders.

"You must not speak out of turn," Amyya said quickly. "It is dangerous."

But Redheart was not to be deterred. "Esteemed Elders," she said loudly, urgently, struggling to keep her voice above the tumult washing around the theatre. "Please hear me. I beg you!"

The Head Elder raised a hand and bellowed a single word: "Silence!"

The crowd obeyed, but not instantly. Slowly their voices drifted away, and the Elder pointed at Redheart.

"Very well. I will hear what you have to say." Her voice carried an unmistakable warning. "But you, Queen Amyya, will not translate for your people."

Under the scrutiny of every Ulyyn more now than ever, Redheart looked at Amyya's concerned face, and then licked her lips nervously.

"I do not know what threat Dun-Wyrd could pose to your mighty queendom," she said to the Elders with careful respect, "but if we join to rid the Great Forest of her presence, Prince Kyjah will be returned to you."

The Head Elder scoffed. "I am not easily fooled, Woman of Boska. You speak of our prince yet your thoughts linger on the son of your Duchess." She cut Redheart off before the knight could reply. "For more than a century, no Ulyyn has strayed from the borders of Uljah, but the Spirits of the Forest can see Kyjah nowhere in our lands. If what you have told us is true, human, then Kyjah has failed his rite of passage, failed his people, and he is unworthy of the title king. The Ulyyn abandon him."

"Then what of the leaf talisman?" Redheart said quickly, desperately. "I'm told it grants one favour."

"And death."

"Then I accept that death," Redheart stated proudly. "For the son of my duchess, for the son of your queen, I give my life in return for your help."

The audience, who could only understand the Head Elder's side of the exchange, seemed to glean that this stranger from a different land had made some kind of grand gesture. Whispers rose among them.

Amyya looked at Redheart with a curious expression on her small face. "You... you would do this?"

"Gladly," Redheart assured her.

"Be careful with your words, Woman of Boska." The Head Elder's voice was hard, irreproachable. "Your saving grace is that you do not understand our culture. You were deceived by the accursed feliwyrd. The talisman belongs to Abildan, and it is not your place to exploit it. To think otherwise is an insult to the Spirits of the Forest, so I suggest that you keep your pride behind your teeth."

Amyya laid a hand on Redheart's shoulder, her small fingers digging in meaningfully. "Say no more," she warned.

The Elder address the queen, her tone remaining harsh. "Queen Amyya, you will escort our intruder to our borders and banish her from these lands." She pointed at Redheart. "And know this, Woman of Boska, should you ever seek to return to Uljah, then it will be as Uljah's enemy."

She banged the wooden ball against the armrest. "The Elders have spoken. The council is ended."

The Ulyyn broke into a mass of chattering voices. Redheart looked to Amyya, but the queen did not look back at her. Her eyes were glazed, staring off into an unknown distance. Mettle and determination decorated her face.

Eighteen
Dark Magic

Morning came with an overcast sky that reduced the sun to a smudge of weak light behind heavy clouds, grey and miserable. Drizzle misted the air and clung to the chill of night. It beaded upon Vladisal's tarnished armour.

She and her remaining thirteen knights and five archers hid just inside the tree line where the forest broke to reveal a large glade of wild grass. The glade appeared lush, and should have smelled sweet in the spring rain; but the sickly scent of decay was rife, and an unseen menace hung as heavy as the grey clouds above.

Vladisal narrowed her eyes.

Ahead of the company, out in the open, Abildan sat cross-legged upon the wet grass. She had that sack which Vladisal had seen her with the previous day. What contents it might hold, the feliwyrd was in no hurry to reveal, and she sat in a meditative state – praying, perhaps, to whichever dark gods she worshipped.

To Vladisal's left, old Üban stamped her feet against the cold. "A miserable day to end a miserable quest," she muttered.

Not one woman among them had slept during the night – no one dared to, not in the aftermath of Dun-Wyrd's sinister visit. Poor Sir Mervya; she had succumbed to the damnation of the Bone Shaker's foul magic, and Vladisal had given her spirit peace. Her dead body had been laid to rest upon a pyre, along with the bodies of Sir Finn, Sir Theodora and Sir Brennik. In a hollow voice, Vladisal had recited prayers to the Mother God while the dead burned and the living mourned.

After that, the night had been long and tense, but there had been nothing to do except wait for dawn when Abildan had led the company to the glade. At least no other knight had been stung by a tree-demon.

What paths have I led you down, my friends? Vladisal wondered, and she could not find the courage to turn and face the brave women congregated behind her.

With a heavy spirit, Vladisal risked a glance at the grey and expressionless face of Luca standing on her right. Luca kept her eyes fixed on Abildan, as if reluctant to look at her friend. Vladisal wished she could find words of strength to comfort Luca's heartbreak – and Üban's and her own - but there was nothing she could say that could undo what was done.

An attempt had been made to find Dief, but the night's mist had grown too thick in the forest, and it was unwise to stray far from camp. Vladisal had eventually ordered the women to abandon their search. A hard decision that had to be made. They all understood that finding Dief would have made little difference to the outcome. She had been infected by tree-demons, cursed by the damned. Vladisal knew Dief too well, as did Üban and especially Luca. She had wished to end her life in solitude, with dignity, while she was still able to recognise friend from foe.

From the ache in her heart and the expressions on the faces of her knights, Vladisal respected that the manner in which they had lost their sisters would haunt all their dreams for years to come.

"By the Mother," Üban whispered. "Is… Is that a spider?"

She was watching Abildan. The feliwyrd had taken from the sack an enormous spider, easily the size of a dog. It lay dead on its back, legs curled against its body almost defensively.

"What's she doing with it?" Luca said.

It was difficult to tell at first, for Abildan had positioned herself between the spider and the knights. By the look of things, she was breaking off the spider's legs, one by one. When all eight were removed and thrown aside, Abildan drew her sabre and sliced into the bloated, black body. She twisted her position to give a better view of what she was doing.

Luca made a noise of disgust. Abildan had pushed a hand inside the spider. She searched around for a moment before cutting out a dark, dripping mass, which she proceeded to eat.

More sounds of loathing and disgust came from the women behind Vladisal.

Üban hawked and spat on the ground. "Blood magic," she growled. "Is this really what we've come to?"

"The hours is late, and Redheart has not returned with the Ulyyn," Vladisal said in a resigned but strong voice. "We few are all that stand in

Dun-Wyrd's way, and we must hope that it is enough."

"We stand with you, Vlad," Luca said. "For Elander, for Duchess Mayland, for... absent friends."

"Aye, lass," Üban agreed, and a seed of dark mirth crept into her tone. "But if it's all the same to you two, I'll be praying the Bone Shaker is not as hard a foe as the feliwyrd would have us believe. There's a keg of ale and one or two bachelors waiting for me at Mayland Castle."

A sad smile came to Luca's face. Vladisal could not prevent a sombre chuckle escaping her lips. These were fine women she stood beside, the best.

Abildan had finished her grisly meal. She sprang to her feet, as if energised. With her back to the company, she stretched her arms out wide to encompass the glade. She spoke unintelligible words that came from all places, borne on the rain.

"Here we go," Vladisal said, and she turned to her knights, issuing the order to bear arms.

When Abildan finished speaking in a sorcerous tongue, the air shifted and a low hum passed through the company like a charged breeze before a storm. The light dimmed over the glade. The clouds grew fatter and darker. And where nothing but wild grassland had stretched before the knights, a structure began to materialise in the glade.

Murmurs of consternation rose, voices on the verge of panic.

Vladisal wheeled around, slicing a hand through the air for order. "Prepare yourselves!" she said, and the knights fell back into an edgy silence, gripping their weapons tightly.

The structure continued to gain substance before Abildan's outstretched arms, and soon became as real and solid as the trees surrounding the glade. It was a simply designed fort, comprising four broad walls made from dark, hard-packed earth, veined with thick roots, easily four times the height any women. It looked as though it has risen from the ground itself.

The lair of Dun-Wyrd.

The entrance was a wide arch cut into the front facing wall. A courtyard could be seen through it. However, there was no ungodly horde of tree-demons waiting to attack the Boskan knights. No Bone Shaker to receive them.

"Where's our reception party?" Üban said, with no small measure of surprise in her voice.

"This place looks deserted," Luca said.

Vladisal frowned. "Walk with me, my friends."

The three of them approached Abildan, leaving the rest of the women in the trees.

With the ruins of the dead spider at her feet, the feliwyrd stared at the lair. Her eyes were no longer yellow, but black and shiny like the shell of a beetle. Blood matted the fur on her face and she radiated an unnatural energy. She didn't acknowledge the knights standing between her and the lair.

"Well, feliwyrd?" Üban said, "Have we caught your countrywoman unawares?"

"Unlikely," Abildan replied.

"Why does this place feel so deserted?" Vladisal asked. "Has Dun-Wyrd moved location?"

"Quite possibly."

Üban growled. "Perhaps she fled in fear of us."

Abildan's yellow eyes fixed on her. "Again, unlikely." She looked at her hands, as if contemplating the power of blood magic. Claws slid from her fingertips, and then retracted. "I cannot feel Dun-Wyrd's magic. But that does not mean she has fled. It does not mean she is here, either. A Wyrd could easily hide her presence from us."

"A trap?" Vladisal said.

"Quite possibly." Abildan motioned to the lair's arched entranceway. "Shall we go and find out?"

With a nod from Vladisal, Luca signalled to the waiting knights to follow. They emerged from the trees, and Abildan led the company into the Bone Shaker's lair.

The courtyard was square, roughly fifty paces wide and long, only marginally less bland than the exterior. Crudely carved stairs led up to ramparts on the left and right walls. Sitting at the centre was a smaller structure with a flat roof, resembling a simple mausoleum. The entire lair was fashioned from hard, root-veined earth. It looked like a child had built a clumsy, oversized dirt model of a fortress.

"Archers," Vladisal ordered, motioning to the ramparts. "Cover the courtyard."

Without hesitation, the archers did as their captain ordered. Two took the steps to the left wall, three ascended to the right. The remaining knights spread out in the courtyard. Vladisal, Üban and Luca stayed close to the feliwyrd.

Abildan approached the crude mausoleum and tilted her head as she stared into its small and darkened doorway. Vladisal strained to see for herself through the doorway, but her eyes could not penetrate the gloom.

"What do you see, Abildan?"

"Stairs leading down."

"Too where?"

"A dark place." Abildan's eyes glinting blackly. "We each of us have our duty to perform, yes?"

"Aye, that we do," Üban said wryly.

Abildan gave the old knight a crooked smile. "Perceptions of duty tend to alter when you do not expect to survive, do they not?"

Üban smirked. "It does add an interesting flavour, I'll admit."

"Welcome to my world, Sir Knight." Abildan considered the doorway again. "If Dun-Wyrd is still here, then she is hiding deep down beneath us, and that is where she will also be keeping Elander."

Upon hearing this, Luca turned the Vladisal, "Shall I gather the women? Half of us to search - the rest to guard the courtyard."

"No," Abildan said. "This is a Wyrd's lair. A labyrinth of narrow burrows and corridors awaits at the bottom of those stairs, with little room for a company of knights to manoeuvre. Sir Vladisal and I will go alone."

"Not bloody likely," Üban snapped.

"Wait," Vladisal said. "Explain yourself, Abildan."

"I know the mind of the Wyrd, ladies." The feliwyrd wiped spider blood from her chin. "Who among us stands a chance against magic better than I? Leading your woman down into the bowels of the lair might just lead them to slaughter."

Blood magic had given Abildan a strange and menacing calm. If there was any deceit left in the feliwyrd, any treachery at all, she had not reserved it for this moment.

"We have trusted you this far, Abildan," Vladisal said. "Let us do this your way."

"You cannot be serious!" Üban said. "What if you find the Bone Shaker and a legion of tree-demons?"

"She's right, Vlad," Luca added. "At least let Üban and I go with you."

Vladisal and Abildan stared at each other for a moment.

"No," Vladisal said resolutely. "You two command the women in my absence." She stopped Üban arguing further by gripping the old knight's shoulder. "Hear your captain, my friend, and trust her. If ill befalls me, then Elander is relying on you."

Both of them were reluctant to move. Abildan walked into the mausoleum's entrance and waited in the shadows.

"Go to the women," Vladisal ordered her knights. "Keep them alert," and she followed Abildan into depths of darkness.

Nineteen
The Lair of the Boneshaker

The stairs were steep, descending sharply into the ground, into a lightless void. Soon, Vladisal was swamped by utter darkness and couldn't see her hand before her face.

"Hold still," Abildan said.

The Boskan Captain flinched as the rough pad of assassin's hand covered her eyes.

An alien word was whispered. Vladisal felt its unnatural energy scraping the inside of her skull, prickling at her mind. She gasped and staggered on the stairs. Abildan held her steady, and when the she removed her hand, Vladisal could see in the dark. The feliwyrd and the stairs were revealed, tinged with ghostly green.

"Come," Abildan said.

Vladisal followed her down the stairs, desperately trying to ignore the incongruous feel of blood magic.

It took a surprisingly long time to reach the bottom of the lair. They followed a long corridor, neatly carved into the earth. It was narrow, and they walked single file, passing many other corridors that split off to the left and right. Vladisal realised that Abildan had spoken the truth. There wasn't room enough to swing a sword. The Bone Shaker's lair was a labyrinth of pitch dark tunnels which formed no kind of ground on which a company of knights could stand and fight.

"How long has Dun-Wyrd been in the Great Forest?" Vladisal whispered to her guide. "It must have taken her an age to create this place."

"Magic has many uses," Abildan said without looking back. "A lair such as this would be a simple work for a Wyrd. But it's a temporary structure. Its purpose served."

Now the feliwyrd mentioned it, the walls and low ceiling did look dry and cracked, the floor crumbling underfoot. Dust laced the air and scratched the back of Vladisal's throat. A vague stench of rotting foliage came to her nose. It was as though the lair was dying.

They approached the corridor's end where two paths split left and right. Abildan brought them to a halt before they reached the junction. She cocked her ear, listening. Vladisal heard it too: soft whining – a dog, perhaps - but she couldn't tell from which direction it came.

Abildan crept forward, claws sliding from fingertips as she turned left, leading Vladisal to the doorway of a chamber, where a pack of wolves were held captive.

There were ten of them at least. Most cowered against the back wall. Two paced and whined. But one, braver than the others, stood close to the doorway, teeth bared and hackles raised, growling at the intruders. To Vladisal's altered vision, its eyes shone green in the dark.

The wolf barked and leapt to attack. Vladisal jumped aside. Abildan stood her ground, merely observing as the wolf hit some invisible barrier covering the doorway. With a snapping sound and a spark like a knife had struck flint, the wolf yelped and recoiled, scurried off to cower with the pack, pawing at its snout.

Abildan reach out and tapped a claw againsy the magical barrier. A ripple like water spread over the doorway. "I told you that Dun-Wyrd was happy for you to come to her." She turned black eyes to her companion. "You have heard tales of the caniwyrd?"

Vladisal nodded. "The dog-soldiers of Mya-Siad. Yes, Üban has fought them."

"How ironic." Abildan snorted. "Hyena make the best specimen of caniwyrd, for their survival mechanisms are second to none. However, a wolf will create just as fierce a warrior, especially if its spirit has been merged with a trained knight."

Vladisal stared into the chamber, at the pack of frightened wolves, and she felt cold.

"Take a good look, Sir Vladisal. Should Dun-Wyrd prevail, these wolves are your future." Abildan's lip curled into a snarl or smile, Vladisal couldn't tell which. "And their presence is a sure sign that Dun-Wyrd is still here."

Before Vladisal had time to think or speak, a moan drifted down the dark tunnel.

It had been a human voice - emotional, not the empty, tormented tone of a tree-demon. It sounded again, from somewhere in the lair, and this time Vladisal was positive that it belonged to a youngster. A boy.

"Elander."

Abildan was facing in the opposite direction to the voice, stock still and tense.

"Magic…" Her claws slid back into her fingers. "My duty is to kill Dun-Wyrd. Elander is your responsibility." She unhooked the single-handed crossbow from her belt. "Good luck, Sir Vladisal."

Abildan's image blurred and sped off at preternatural speed.

"Wait!" Vladisal shouted.

But the feliwyrd had already disappeared into the far gloom which even heightened sight could not penetrate. Blood magic crackled in the air. The wolves stirred in their pen.

The voice drifted down the corridor again. This time, Vladisal fancied that she heard Elander call her name. Alone and desperate, she ran towards it. The wolves howled behind her.

Twenty
Sunshine

Drizzle had turned to hard rain.

The courtyard offered no cover, and the knights braved the weather. Üban tried to ignore the cold droplets that drummed upon her armour and trickled down her neck. She and Luca walked the perimeter of the courtyard, their metal boots squelching in the shallow layer of mud on the ground. The rest of the women were spread out, swords in hands, while archers guarded from the ramparts, watching for whatever surprises might disturb this strange stillness.

In the distance, thunder rumbled.

"We should have gone with her," Luca grumbled as she and Üban came in line with the doorway to the mausoleum. "How long do you think we should give them?"

Üban rolled her eyes. This was not the first time that Luca had voiced her concerns since Vladisal had gone off with Abildan.

"You know, I once met Vlad's father," Üban said. "He was a good man, a strong man, but he never stopped worrying about his daughter. You and he do not sound dissimilar."

But Luca was in no mind to entertain the old knight's attempt to lighten the mood. "We've lost enough friends on this quest." Her voice was bitter, her expression dark. "I don't like all this waiting around."

Üban sighed. She didn't much like the inaction, either, but what else could they do? If the Bone Shaker wasn't here, which seemed likely, what did that mean? Could they trust Abildan to find Dun-Wyrd again? Could she do it in time to save Elander?

Shrugging off fatigue and a growing sense of misery, Üban slapped Luca on the arm. "Remember that barrel of ale I told you about? When we get home, I'll share it with you. We'll drink to Dief."

Luca nodded. "Dief would like that." She managed a smile. "But you know what, right now I'd pay real gold just for a good fire and the shelter of a sturdy oak."

Üban grinned, but her chuckle died in her throat as the rain stopped so suddenly it was as though it had been stolen from the sky.

The heavy, grey clouds began clearing. One by one, they evaporated, allowing spears of brilliant sunshine to come piercing through. In but a moment, the sky above the courtyard was clear and dazzling blue. Worried murmurs rose from the knights as the sun bathed them in its warm, golden glow.

"This is not nature's work," Üban said.

Unholy energy charged the air.

Cries of alarm came from the women. A figure had appeared, standing on the flat roof of the mausoleum. Head bald, body thin and hunched, she was dressed in dark robes. Her hands were raised to the sun, and her voice whispered around the courtyard with sorcerous menace.

Luca swore.

"Dun-Wyrd..."

A rumble, like a giant bellowing in the bowels of the earth, shook the ground. A wall of hard dirt rose to block the lair's arched entrance, trapping the knights in the courtyard.

"Form ranks!" Üban shouted.

But the order had barely passed her lips when the sodden ground began to churn and a hand gripped her leg.

Twenty-One
Old Friend

With vision aided by magic, Vladisal sped through the labyrinthine network of dark corridors, the twists and turns tinged with green, the way guided by Elander's soft calls. The Boskan captain focussed her every thought, her every instinct on reaching the son of her Duchess and spiriting him away from the terrible gloom of Dun-Wyrd's lair.

Elander's voice led her into a corridor where mist glowed with pale blue radiance, hovering a foot or more above the ground. Vladisal slowed her pace. The mist swirled as she crept through it. A moan came from directly ahead, where the tunnel ended at the doorway to a chamber.

Vladisal ran forward.

Inside the chamber, the mist reached halfway up her thighs. A person, shrouded in blue radiance, lay curled on the floor by the back wall. Vladisal's heart pounded, but instinct stopped her rushing to the person. Instead, she took a cautious step backward.

"Elander?"

The figure stirred and stood. Large and thickset, much bigger than the young boy Vladisal championed.

A woman wearing tarnished armour rose out of the mist. Her head was shaven close to the scalp, and in her hands was a mighty war hammer.

Vladisal's world grew infinitely narrower.

"Dief?"

Face twitching at the sound of the voice, Dief's eyes remained closed, as though she slept. "Vlad?" Her voice was whispery, distant. "Is that you?"

Vladisal swallowed. "I am here, my friend."

"I'm sorry, my captain. I tried to end my life in the forest, but she called..." Dief opened her eyes; they glowed with the same blue light as the mist. "Her voice was strong, inside my veins. She brought me here and made me understand her vision."

Vladisal adopted a defensive stance. "Dief, what has the Bone Shaker done to you?" She drew her sword.

"Showed me the future." Dief coughed and gagged. "And you have no part in Dun-Wyrd's vision." She lofted the war hammer. "Forgive me..."

"Wait!" Vladisal snapped, but the big knight did not hear her.

With a roar of rage and hate, Dief rushed forward, swinging the hammer. Vladisal barley managed to dodge the blow, slashing out with her sword. The hammer easily parried the strike. She spun around Dief, further into the chamber, and managed to put a little distance between them.

"Dief, wait!" Vladisal begged. "You are not yourself. There is magic-"

Dief gave no respite. All humanity lost to her, she charged again.

Vladisal forgot all memory of friendship, and sliced at her neck. But Dief moved with unnatural speed and blocked the sword with the hammer's long handle, before swinging for her captain once again. Vladisal's blade met the attack. The force of the blow sent numbing shockwaves up her arm, and the sword fell clattering from her hand, lost in the mist. Vladisal tried to dodge the next strike, but the hammer smashed into her breastplate, sending her crashing into the back wall.

With a groan, Vladisal slid down into a sitting position. She coughed blood onto her chin. Dief loomed over her, face grim and eyes glowing.

"My captain." A root slid from Dief's mouth, its tip probing her face. "Farewell."

"No-" Blood choked off Vladisal's plea. She could only watch the hammer rise above her.

Dief grunted as her head snapped forward and back again. Her face creased with pain. She turned from Vladisal. A crossbow bolt was buried in the back of her head.

In the doorway, Abildan calmly drew the string of her crossbow, selected a new bolt from her baldric, and slid it into place.

Dief screamed with a demon's curse that seemed to shake the very foundations of the lair. The feliwyrd sent the second bolt into her face.

The way Dief rocked on her feet, it was though she had been struck by a sudden thought rather than a bolt from a crossbow. She tried to take a step, faltered, and dropped to her knees. The war hammer hit the floor with a dull clang. Through swirling mists, Abildan pounced, sabre in hand. Silent, with an utter lack of emotion on her feline face, she hacked at Dief's thick neck – once, twice, three times before her head tumbled to the floor and her body fell to one side.

Abildan crouched beside Vladisal and placed a hand on her dented breastplate, muttering words of a dark and sorcerous tongue.

White fire sank into Vladisal's chest and she yelled in pain. She felt broken ribs mend, damaged organs repair. She coughed more blood, and then the pain eased and was gone completely.

Abildan helped her to her feet with a smirk. "That's twice I've saved your life now, Sir Knight. Such a shame you probably won't survive to repay your debt."

Vladisal placed a hand against her dented breastplate. She looked down at Dief's body in the mist and swallowed her grief. "I take it your search was fruitless."

"Quite." Abildan reclaimed the sword from beneath Dief's leg and gave it to the knight. "I can feel Dun-Wyrd's magic, but…" She closed her eyes and cursed. "Of course. The Melding Arc."

"What is it?" Vladisal said.

Abildan cursed again. "To fuse the spirit of Elander with an Ulyyn, Dun-Wyrd will utilise a device called the Melding Arc. To power this device, she needs the light of the sun-"

Abildan cocked her ear, listening to something beyond Vladisal's hearing range. She bared her pointed teeth.

"It seems that we must work together after all, Sir Vladisal." She headed for the door. "Do try to keep up."

Twenty-Two
Old Enemies

Tree-demons besieged the Knights of Boska. Dun-Wyrd surveyed the pandemonium.

Her army rose from the ground, clambering free of the earth, churning flat terrain into a rough and treacherous battlefield. Trapped in the courtyard, fighting beneath a brilliant sun, the knights rallied with brave hearts. But the tree-demons came as thick as ants spilling from an anthill. Protected by coils of armoured wood, poisonous roots whipping from their mouths, they met the knights with a single purpose.

The mergings hungered for blood, but they would not feed, would not infect. Not today. Dun-Wyrd wanted these women of Boska captured.

Up on the mausoleum roof, the Bone Shaker had cast a magical barrier. Translucent energy wavered gently in the air, and sound struggled to pass through it. The tumult of battle was nothing more than a dull and distant noise. These knights had already proved themselves to be clever and pragmatic, and Dun-Wyrd would take no risks with her plans.

Turning from the battle, she inspected the progress of the Melding Arc.

The fat stone body hovered on its back. Its doors were open, the magic in its belly exposed to the sun. The spell was nearing completion. Greedily, it drank natural energy from the pure and golden rays. Earlier, Dun-Wyrd had watched the magic swell, and two vaporous, tentacle-like arms had burst from the green radiance, first reaching for the sky before coiling tightly around the two captives who stood immobile on either side of the Melding Arc.

Elander remained unconscious. His young features were slack, lined by tendrils of lank, raven hair. Prince Kyjah, however, openly stared at his captor. His expression appeared defiant, but the Dun-Wyrd could see the fear hiding in his eyes.

"Not long now, little prince," Dun-Wyrd promised him. "Soon, none of this will matter to you."

Kyjah spoke in his native tongue: a single click followed by a harsh grunt. Dun-Wyrd understood the Ulyyn language and recognised the insult. She smiled at the boy's bravado.

A dull ticking, followed by a snapping sound, distracted the Wyrd.

Boskan archers were loosing arrows upon her. But they could not hit their mark. Each arrow shattered upon the invisible barrier, causing it to waver and spark, before they dissolved to energy that was absorbed by the magic. It would take much more than mundane projectiles to stop Dun-Wyrd. Still, she was irritated by the audacity of the archers, so she pulsed a command to her tree-demons, ordering them to climb the stairs to the ramparts and put an end to their petty attacks.

Down below, the knights fought with ferocity and skill, but they were heavily outnumbered. Dun-Wyrd had culled the entire population of three villages to create her army. They might have been slow and lumbering, but they pressed the attack with no regard to defence, and they were many.

Like a plague, the tree-demons spread across the courtyard, strangling the knights' manoeuvring room. The weapons of the Boskans were fast becoming useless, and for each foe they cut down, more pressed in on every woman.

Dun-Wyrd's eye was drawn to the oldest knight on the battlefield, the one they called Üban. She fought especially hard; she was obviously well-trained and canny enough to reserve her strength. She would make a fine caniwyrd - an obvious choice for pack leader. The archers were useless to Dun-Wyrd's needs. The tree-demons could feed upon their blood. The rest, once merged with the spirits of wolves, would make seasoned warriors. A vicious and loyal personal guard.

Even as she relished this thought, Dun-Wyrd narrowed her eyes and cast her gaze further over the courtyard. There would always be at least one irritating loose end to tie up.

Abildan.

The feliwyrd was nowhere to be seen, but she was close by, somewhere. Dun-Wyrd could feel the taint of blood magic in the air. Abildan was too skilled to be blindsided by the little surprise that Dun-

Wyrd had left in the labyrinth below the lair, but she wasn't so strong that she could deny her breeding, ignore the calling in her blood.

Dun-Wyrd gave a thin smile.

She would break Abildan's conditioning, force her to abandon the orders of Mya-Siad, and... well, a feliwyrd would make a handy servant for what was to come.

Sobbing.

Elander had awoken. His eyes were filled with tears and terror as he stared at the coils of green magic holding his arms to his body. He noticed the Melding Arc, looked at stoic Prince Kyjah on the other side, and finally his eyes found Dun-Wyrd's.

"Please," he begged between sobs. "Let me go."

"Rejoice," Dun-Wyrd told him. "You cannot yet imagine the wonders you will see."

Elander fell into uncontrollable weeping. Kyjah glared with loathing.

At that moment, the sun completed its work. The Melding Arc activated. The spell flared and droned, pulsing with bursts of emerald that spun around the captives, and the merging of their spirits began.

Twenty-Three
For Mya-Siad

Abildan ran from the mausoleum into bright sunshine and chaos. The desperate shouts of fighting women mingled with the emotionless groans of tree-demons. The wet chopping of sharp metal against soft flesh and pulpy wood smacked around the courtyard like a busy day in a butcher's shop.

Abildan headed through the chaos with no thought for helping the knights. Her blood magic had already weakened; she had not expected the healing of Vladisal's wounds to drain so much power. The feliwyrd had neither the strength nor time to fight a hopeless battle alongside these frantic women.

The battlefield was now as treacherous as a freshly ploughed field. Already, a few knights were buried beneath groups of tree-demons, whose roots and claws scratched and pulled at armour. The rest were surrounded by animated corpses, the room to swing a sword slowly diminishing. But the tree-demons were not trying to feed; they were harvesting the women of Boska, preparing them for Dun-Wyrd's experiments.

And the Wyrd herself was up on the mausoleum roof, surveying her work.

Abildan needed higher ground, and fast.

The tree-demons paid the small assassin little mind as she dodged and weaved, nimble footed, running in a blur of blood magic. They were too focussed on the knights. Sir Üban noticed her, though.

"Abildan!" the old knight roared. "Where is Vladisal?"

The feliwyrd kept running, but risked a glance back.

Beside Üban, Sir Luca slipped and fell. A horde of tree-demon's descended on her. Üban herself was on her knees, clearly exhausted, swinging her sword at her foes with clumsily, tired strokes.

"Help us, you bastard!"

Abildan ignored her. Üban bellowed like a beast. Tree-demons swarmed and her voice fell silent.

Wending her way along the lair's right side wall, Abildan side-stepped two children fighting over the bloody remains of an archer, and she bounded up the steps to the rampart.

Ahead, the narrow path was littered with tree-demons feeding upon two more archers. Clearly, Dun-Wyrd had no interest in using them to create her caniwyrd. With supernatural speed and agility, Abildan vaulted and danced, until she was clear of the monsters. She drew level with the mausoleum and stopped.

Dun-Wyrd stood with her back to the feliwyrd, supervising the Melding Arc and the two captives connected to it. Elander and an Ulyyn boy were limp in the grasp of green, pulsing magic that fed a swollen spell like a mighty jewel. The Melding Arc had activated. Soon, these children would be joined to create an oracwyrd.

Abildan unhooked the crossbow from her belt and drew back then string. Dropping to one knee, she laid the weapon aside and reached inside her jerkin for the slim, wooden box she had carried all the way from Mya-Siad.

The black bolt lay inside. The silver, conical head glinted in the sunlight. Abildan took it out with a steady hand and slid it into the groove of the crossbow.

Using the last of the blood magic, she breathed upon the bolt, ruffling the grey feathers of its flight. The magical symbols and words engraved into the spiralling blade began to glow. Dark vapour rose from it like smoke from a candle. The bolt vibrated in the crossbow, eager to be loosed. Abildan took aim at Dun-Wyrd's back.

"For Mya-Siad," she breathed and pulled the trigger.

The bolt flew across the courtyard, high above the battle, whining, trailing dark smoke. With a sharp snap of lightning, it struck the magical barrier surrounding the mausoleum's roof. The air rippled like water, the bolt appearing to be stuck in nothing. A heartbeat passed, and then the bolt began to turn, its spiralling blade screwing into Dun-Wyrd's magic.

The Bone Shaker turned in surprise. She took a moment to stare at the projectile drilling into her defences, before looking across at the rampart to give Abildan a baleful glare. She raised a hand. The air shimmered as she added more power to the barrier.

The bolt stopped as though it had become lodged in midair.

A brief look of disdain passed over Dun-Wyrd's face as she turned back to the Melding Arc.

The tree-demons lost all interest in the dead archers. Their glowing eyes turned to Abildan. She dropped the crossbow and drew her sabre. The blood magic was spent. The tree-demons shuffled towards her.

"Things will pass as the oracwyrd foresee," Abildan muttered coldly.

She leapt into battle with a yowl of defiance.

Twenty-Four
For Boska

Vladisal took the wide and uneven steps two, three at a time, rising from the bowels of the lair to the mausoleum roof. When fresh air and warm sunshine hit her, she became aware that something was wrong with the atmosphere.

She saw Abildan fighting on the rampart. She saw her knights fighting for their lives down in the courtyard. They were losing. There were tree-demons everywhere. But the sounds that reached Vladisal's ears were dampened, distant. The air rippled and fizzed with magic.

Her breath caught when her eyes found Elander.

He was unconscious, held by more magic, pulsing and flaring, connecting him to a strange contraption of stone. The Melding Arc, Abildan had called it; and, just as the feliwyrd had predicted, an Ulyyn boy had also been connected to it. Vladisal knew little of supernatural ways, but judging by the way the Melding Arc's drone was rising in pitch it was preparing to merge the spirits of two children.

The Ulyyn was staring at Vladisal. With a nod of his head, he drew the knight's attention to something behind him.

Seething hatred boiled in Vladisal's soul.

Hunched and withered, Dun-Wyrd stood with her back to the Melding Arc, studying what appeared to be a crossbow bolt stuck in midair. Vladisal's lip curled. She raised her sword and charged the Bone Shaker.

Dun-Wyrd twitched. Her hand shot out.

Energy hit Vladisal's chest, punching her onto her back. The sword clattered from her grasp. She lay gasping, gaping at the sky. The sound of fighting seemed to come from a dreamlike place. Dun-Wyrd's shadow fell across her.

The Bone Shaker lowered her hood, revealing a skeletal face and a head shaved smooth. For a moment, she seemed amused by the Boskan knight at her feet. But then she expressed pity and finally hatred.

Dazed, Vladisal tried to reclaim her sword. With another flicker of magic, Dun-Wyrd numbed all feeling in Vladisal's arms and legs.

"At least you'll die knowing that you tried," the Bone Shaker said.

Vladisal sank back, looking at the Melding Arc.

The spell inside the stone body was growing and bubbling, threatening to spill over as if the green magical energy was viscous fluid boiling in a pot. Elander and the Ulyyn boy were shaking, mouths open and eyes closed. Magic swept between them in dazzling flashes, feeding their spirits into the Melding Arc. Elander would soon be lost forever. His champion had failed him, failed her women.

Sensing the last vestiges of hope vanish, praying to the Mother God, Vladisal gritted her teeth. "I'll kill you," she hissed at Dun-Wyrd.

The Bone Shaker shook her head in bemusement. She raised her hand, summoning the dark magic that would destroy Vladisal.

A cry from above stopped her.

Shadows descended from the sky. More cries came. At first, Vladisal couldn't see past the glare of the sun, but she quickly realised that the shadows were birds, hawks of gigantic size, and they came one after the other, too many to count. Warriors rode on the backs of the hawks, armed with spears and bows, swooping down upon the lair. It took Vladisal a moment to comprehend what she was seeing. A surge of hope filled her.

"The Ulyyn."

Dun-Wyrd's gaunt face creased with rage. She turned from Vladisal and approached the Melding Arc. Elander and the Ulyyn boy were suffused with an emerald glow.

The feeling returned to Vladisal's limbs. She jumped to her feet and retrieved her sword, ducking as a giant hawked low dived over the mausoleum. A woman sat behind the diminutive Ulyyn rider, a woman in armour that glinted in the sunlight. Vladisal's spirits soared.

"Redheart!"

The Ulyyn jumped from the hawk's back as it passed over the roof. Magic crackled and snapped as she passed through whatever barrier had been cast over the mausoleum. She landed gracefully, and the hawk carried Redheart away.

A host of warriors jumped from the backs of giant birds, landing down in the courtyard, and an army of Forest Dwellers joined the fight against the tree-demons.

The Ulyyn woman crouched, her hands pressed flat to the roof. Her hair styled into a topknot, a red and gold torc around her neck, she carried no weapon but the look she aimed at the Bone Shaker was filled with a tempest.

Dun-Wyrd summon her magic. The Ulyyn summoned hers.

She spoke in a quick tongue, clicks and grunts that didn't sound like language. Dun-Wyrd, her face panicked, chanted silently, her bony fingers weaving intricate symbols in the air.

Elander and the boy shook in the coils of the Melding Arc's tentacles. The spell was rising, its colour darkening.

The voice of the Ulyyn woman rose in volume.

A tremor shook the mausoleum. Vladisal staggered, and so did Dun-Wyrd.

Clearly struggling to combat her adversary's magic, the Bone Shaker couldn't prevent cracks appearing in the roof. The ground shook. The mausoleum groaned. Mighty roots, as thick as arms, slithered out from the ever widening cracks. They shot up into the air, swaying and writhing like the tentacles of some great beast risen from the depths of the hells. As one, they reached for Dun-Wyrd.

She met the attack with surprising agility for one so bent and withered. Fire blazed from her quick hands, reducing serpentine root after serpentine root to ash. But more came, rising from the cracks in the roof. Tremors continued to shake the ground, and Dun-Wyrd did not realise that her barrier had been weakened.

The crossbow bolt began turning in the air, drilling its way forward, faster and faster.

The Ulyyn woman sent a root to stab at the Melding Arc. Wood burned and smoked. The spell paled a little.

While Dun-Wyrd was occupied by her serpentine foes, the bolt drilled free of the barrier. Trailing dark vapour, its silver head spinning and shining, the bolt veered, changing direction, and struck Dun-Wyrd in the back.

Her scream was wild, full of dark secrets.

She twisted and turned, desperately trying to reach the sharp blade drilling into her flesh. The remaining roots rose vertically, and slithered down through the cracks, as though fleeing whatever foul magic had beset the Bone Shaker.

The Ulyyn woman rushed to the Melding Arc.

Vladisal remembered the sword in her hand. She strode towards Dun-Wyrd with deadly intent. The Bone Shaker saw her coming and a hissed a curse between her wails. Blood ran down her legs, pooling beneath her feet, spraying as she twisted and turned.

Vladisal raised her sword.

Dun-Wyrd choked on a single word that might have been "No," before she fell, thrashing wildly as black fire engulfed her. The dark flames flared. Vladisal stepped back, turning away from a wash of intense heat that reduced the Bone Shaker to a smouldering pile of blood-coloured ash.

Even as a victory cry rose from the courtyard; even as Vladisal acknowledge that the tree-demons were as dead as their master, she was rushing to Elander's side.

The Ulyyn woman had destroyed the Melding Arc. The spell had vanished, its stone body broken into grey pieces. Elander lay still, and Vladisal gathered him into her arms.

His eyelids fluttered open, and it took him a moment to recognise the face of his champion. "Vlad," he croaked. "I knew you'd come…" And Elander fell unconscious once more.

Vladisal looked to the woman whose help had saved the day. She was cradling the Ulyyn boy's head, gently rocking back and forth as she spoke to him in soft clicks and sighs.

Twenty-Five
Women of Honour

In the glade outside the crumbling lair of the Bone Shaker, the knights of Boska congregated beneath a blanket of grey clouds. Giant hawks circled overhead, some with Ulyyn warriors riding on their backs. Although the sun was hidden, the rains had not returned, the air was warm, and the mood was jubilant.

"By the Mother, you like to cut things fine!" Üban shouted as Redheart joined the company. There was a clash of armour as she pulled her sister into a mighty bear hug. "I'll admit, lass, you had me worried there for a moment."

Redheart laughed. Vladisal shared a grin with Luca.

Dun-Wyrd was dead. Elander was saved.

Ten Boskan women had survived – eleven now Redheart had returned. They stood as a group, celebrating the return of their sister, too euphoric at winning the day to yet mourn those who had fallen in battle; too surprised and relieved to yet acknowledge that they had just been saved by a mythical race who many believed to be extinct.

Redheart had brought at least three score Ulyyn to the battle. Most of the small warriors had remained on the ground, carrying spears and wearing wooden armour. They kept their distance from the knights, watching the celebrations as though witnessing a curious tradition of some unknown species.

Vladisal had not yet spoken to the Ulyyn woman who had changed the tide of the battle. But she had witnessed more of her spells. Calling upon the magic of the Great Forest, she had erected a tent, of a kind. It had risen like a grassy knoll from the very floor on the far side of the glade, next to the tree line. A dark, inverted 'V' served as an entranceway, and inside healers tended to Elander and the Ulyyn boy.

Soon the company would be escorting Elander home to his mother.

As for Abildan, the feliwyrd had not been found among the dead, and no one had seen her. Vladisal wished she had had the chance to thank the cat-like assassin.

"Well, my captain," Redheart said as she escaped Üban's clutches and bowed to Vladisal. "The day is ours."

"Welcome back, old friend." Vladisal clapped Redheart's shoulder, noticing the line of a fresh wound on her face. "I think we had all lost faith that the leaf talisman could help us."

"That thing?" Redheart gave a snort. "Trust me, the talisman isn't worth the wood it's carved from. Not in my hands."

Vladisal frowned.

"There's something you should know, Vlad…"

Redheart trailed off as the gathering of Ulyyn warriors stirred and parted. The woman with the red and gold torc emerged and approached the company, flanked by two armed guards.

Redheart dropped her voice to a whisper. "Her name is Amyya. She is Queen of Uljah."

Amyya… Vladisal remembered the tale that Abildan had told the previous night. The tale of the Ulyyn princess who she had intended to assassinate but had saved instead.

"The boy who was with Elander," Redheart continued. "His name is Kyjah. He's Amyya's son, a prince of the Ulyyn."

Vladisal stepped ahead of her women to meet Amyya with a bow. The other knights followed their captain's lead.

"Your Majesty," Vladisal said. "We offer you our eternal gratitude. Without your help we would have surely perished."

Queen Amyya seemed pleased with the knight's respect, but she did not reply. Instead, she called Redheart forward and addressed her in the Ulyyn tongue. Redheart nodded as if understanding every click and grunt, and then accepted from the queen a little stone of yellow glass.

"Put this in your ear," she said, smiling at her captain's hesitance. "Trust me, my friend."

When Vladisal did as Redheart asked, Amyya spoke again and her words vibrated the stone as if a bee had been trapped in Vladisal ear. She resisted the urge to dig it out and marvelled as the queen's language became a soft, intelligible voice in her mind.

"Your gratitude is well received, Sir Vladisal. As is the chivalry of your knight." She referred pointedly to Redheart. "Elander is strong. He is healed enough to travel home."

"A thousand thanks," Vladisal said, a smile coming unbidden to her face. "House Mayland is truly in your debt."

Amyya drew herself up. "Do not be so quick to say so." Her small face was stern. "At this moment, you and your knights are free to return with Elander to your lands. I urge you to do so. Now."

To return home was exactly what Vladisal wanted, what all the knights wanted, but Amyya spoke as though she was irritated, offended.

"Leave the Great Forest and never think of the feliwyrd again," Amyya added.

"Feliwyrd?" Vladisal looked at Redheart.

"The Ulyyn have Abildan in custody," Redheart explained. "She wants to talk to you, but-"

"That monster is not your responsibility, Sir Vladisal." Amyya regarded her own people, her tawny eyes giving nothing away. "Abildan has much to say for herself, but I will not consider her words until we have taken her back to Uljah. Unless... unless your honour demands that she is heard now."

Vladisal felt the eyes of her knights upon her back. She looked at Redheart, who shrugged, seemingly perplexed.

"Without Abildan, we would not have come very far," Vladisal said uncertainly. "She also deserves our thanks."

"She deserves nothing of the kind," Amyya said, face stony. "I urge you to forget about the feliwyrd."

"With respect, your highness... Elander and your son – they would be dead if not for Abildan. I could not return to Mayland with my honour intact unless my gratitude had been extended to her."

Amyya looked at her guards, at the Ulyyn crowded behind her. They watched their queen silently, expectantly, their small faces full of judgement.

"Very well," Amyya said, resigned, disappointed. "Walk with me, Sir Vladisal. Sir Redheart may accompany you."

She strode off with her guards. The Ulyyn parted to let them through.

Luca stepped up to Vladisal, concerned. "What's this about Abildan?"

"We couldn't understand a bloody word she said," Üban growled.

"I..." Vladisal faltered, aware that the rest of her knights were looking at their captain. Their joy had become tinged with confusion. "Stay with the women," she told Üban and Luca. "Ready them for the journey ahead.

Redheart and I will return shortly."

With Redheart beside her, Vladisal followed Amyya through the crowd of Ulyyn, ignoring the many stern gazes aimed her way.

"What's going on?" she asked her friend. "I believed Abildan was well and truly on her way back to Mya-Siad."

"I don't really understand it myself," Redheart admitted. "These are strange folk, Vlad, and their ways are hard to fathom. Amyya is the Queen of Uljah, but she does not rule the Ulyyn. She has defied her people to rescue her son. This army is her personal guard, loyal to her, but they are not happy that their queen has led them from their lands."

"Abildan told me that she once saved Amyya's life?"

"Yes, that's true." Redheart sighed, casting furtive glances at the Ulyyn. "But it's complicated. The leaf talisman isn't what we thought it was. It belongs to Abildan and no one else. But to use it carries a heavy price. Abildan is both a hero and an enemy, and the talisman cannot be used by anyone but her."

Vladisal pursed her lips. "Then Amyya only came because of her son?"

Redheart nodded. "The Ulyyn way is not our way. Remember that, Vlad."

The two knights cleared the crowd and caught up with Amyya and her guards close to the knoll-like tent, in which Elander received healing. For a moment, Vladisal's spirits soared, suspecting this to be the moment when the boy she had championed since his infancy would be returned to her. But, instead, Amyya called out an order: "Bring her!"

Two Ulyyn warriors appeared from around the tent, ushering forward a prisoner at spear point.

Abildan expressed utter dispassion as she was brought before the queen and the knights. Her wrists were tightly bound by vine rope, and she held in her hands the leaf talisman.

"Sir Vladisal. Sir Redheart." Abildan's yellow eyes turned to Amyya and a smirk appeared on her face. "Queen Amyya. I hear that Prince Kyjah is well and already flying back to Uljah."

"Spare me your mockery and show respect, monster," Amyya snarled. "Or I'll have the tongue cut from your mouth."

The four guards bristled, willing to do more than that with their spears.

Abildan bowed her head, turning the wooden leaf over in her hands as though marvelling at its intricate design. "Curious, isn't it? The talisman granted Sir Redheart no favour from the Ulyyn, yet still they came." She frowned at Vladisal. "Was it then luck that saved the day? Or fate? Did the Wyrd of Mya-Siad foresee everything that has occurred here?"

Vladisal didn't know how to reply at first. There was an air of defeat around the feliwyrd, perhaps resigned to whatever the Ulyyn had in store for her.

"Our alliance has always been troubled," Vladisal said. "There is much trickery in you, Abildan, but, whether by luck or fate, we have all benefitted from your help. And I thank you for that."

Abildan nodded appreciatively, proudly. "You see, your majesty," she said to Amyya. "My actions have favoured both your houses."

"Do not speak to me of favours," the queen said. "I should let these knights strike you down where you stand!"

"But you won't." Abildan held up the leaf talisman. "Because the Spirits of the Forest demand otherwise."

Redheart appeared as nonplussed by the exchange as Vladisal. Loaded, undecipherable meanings passed between the queen and the feliwyrd. Clearly, Amyya wanted dark justice for Abildan's crimes, and yet... did Vladisal have some say in the assassin's fate?

She said, "I don't understand your ways-"

"Nor is it your place to," Amyya snapped. "So be careful with your words, Sir Vladisal."

"A little late for that," Abildan said, slipping into the Ulyyn language. "The queen has broken enough of Uljah's laws, I think." She looked at the warriors guarding her, making sure they understood. "She will not anger the Spirits of the Forest further."

The warriors looked to their queen.

Amyya seethed. She drew a breath. Huffed. Seemed reluctant.

"Sir Vladisal." Her voice was quiet, tremulous in the knight's mind. "The feliwyrd claims that she willingly placed herself in mortal danger to save your life. Is this true?"

"Yes. Twice. Undoubtedly, I wouldn't be standing here if not for Abildan."

"Then you acknowledge that you owe this unworthy abomination a debt of life?"

Vladisal faltered, looked at Redheart, and shrugged. "I do." It was the simple truth.

"Tricks within tricks," Amyya muttered angrily, looking at the ground. "You are free to ask your favour of me, monster."

Triumph came to Abildan's face. "May the Spirits of the Forest be my witness." She lifted the talisman higher, like a trophy. "I call upon the laws of the Ulyyn to recognise my rights. And I demand to be granted this favour."

Abildan's yellow eyes bore into Vladisal. "The debt of life owed to me by Sir Vladisal of House Mayland has been acknowledged. I claim payment. I pass on to her my every crime against Uljah. From this moment, let them be her burden."

A frozen moment.

"What?" said Redheart.

Abildan revealed her canines. "This is the favour that Uljah owes me."

A tear came to Amyya's eye. "The Spirits of the Forest bear witness. So be it."

"Wait," said Vladisal.

But it was too late. The air crackled with magic. The leaf talisman burst into quick flame in Abildan's hands. In an instant, it had been reduced to fine ash that drift away on the forest breeze like a patch of mist. The bonds fell from her wrists.

"Uljah's debt is paid," Amyya said.

Vladisal and Redheart looked at each other in shock, and then at Abildan.

The feliwyrd's smile was cruel. "Üban warned you not to trust me."

"Abildan is free," Amyya told the four warriors. "Secure Sir Vladisal."

Vladisal froze as they leapt forward and two sharp spearheads rested against her throat. Redheart raised her hands as the weapons of the other two warriors steered her away from her captain.

Amyya bellowed a second order across the glade. "Guard the women of Boska!"

"No!" Redheart shouted, but the blades at her throat prevented her from drawing her sword. "Vlad!"

"Be still, Redheart," Vladisal said, as she was urged down to her knees. Her sword was taken and her hands were bound behind her back.

Amyya stood over her, sadness in her eyes, but said nothing as giant hawks cried out and began landing in the glade. The army of Ulyyn had surrounded the small company of knights, spears levelled, too many to fight. But Old Üban shouted a command anyway. She and Luca drew their swords, inspiring others to do the same.

"For the sake of your women, I beg that you do not resist," Amyya said, her tone as hard as steel. "This burden is yours alone and your knights may still return home. Tell them, Sir Vladisal. Tell them now or theirs and Elander's blood will be spilled."

"Stand down!" Vladisal shouted, head spinning with barely conceived understanding, but not doubting the queen's threat for a moment. "Remember your duty to Elander. The oaths you swore to Duchess Mayland. Sheath your weapons!"

"No," Redheart begged. "Not like this. Not for her."

Abildan looked pleased with herself. "I don't suppose my thanks will mean much to you, but I give them nonetheless." She bowed to the knights.

Redheart cursed the injustice of Abildan's final trick. Vladisal glared at the feliwyrd, wishing to skewer her black heart, but knowing that inaction was the only way to ensure the safety of her women.

Behind Abildan, there was movement inside the knoll-like tent. A boy stepped out. Vladisal's breath caught.

Elander.

Dishevelled and grime-smeared, his young face looked concerned, gawping at the giant hawks and the host of Ulyyn warriors surrounding the knights. Überan bellowed another command. The sound of swords sliding back into sheaths rang out. Elander's concern evaporated when her eyes found her champion. Vladisal's heart broke as she watched his joy turned to confusion at why she was held bound and on her knees at spear point.

Abildan noticed the exchange and was amused by it.

"Queen Amyya," said Redheart. "I trusted you. I thought-"

"Take the boy and leave, Sir Redheart," Amyya ordered.

"Vlad?"

"Do as she says," Vladisal growled, trying her best to smile for Elander as he approached. "You lead the women now. No one will resist the Ulyyn. No one will fight for me. Go back to Mayland and return Elander to his mother."

Redheart gave her a pleading look.

"Do as your captain commands," Vladisal snapped. "Now!" Redheart recoiled, and Vladisal softened her tone. "We came here to save the son of our Duchess, my friend, and we have won the day. No more blood will be spilled on my account. I beg you, take Elander home."

"I'd do as she says, if I were you," Abildan said with a bored air.

Redheart bared her teeth. "I'll be seeing you again, feliwyrd."

Yellow eyes flashed. "I'll look forward to it, Sir Knight."

"Vladisal!" Elander was running towards her champion, but the spear of a warrior steered him away and kept him distant.

"Go with Redheart, Elander," Vladisal said, failing to hide the sorrow in her voice. "All will be well."

Redheart put her arm around the boy. Encouraged by the warriors, they made their way back to Überan and Luca and the rest of the knights.

Redheart's eyes locked onto her captain's and she mouthed, "We'll find you."

Vladisal's view of them became blocked when a giant hawk landed with a thump several paces away. There was an Ulyyn rider on its back and wooden cage connected to it by thick vine rope. Two of the warriors unceremoniously dragged Vladisal forward and bundled her into the cage and secured its door.

Amyya stared at Vladisal, her face a stony blank. "You will be taken to Uljah. And there you will stand trial for the feliwyrd's crimes. As for you!" She wheeled on Abildan, snarling. "Be gone from these lands, monster!"

Abildan bowed again. "As you wish."

The Queen of Uljah strode away and disappeared into the tent.

Abildan watched after her and chuckled. "This is a good day."

"I pity you," Vladisal said, gripping the bars of the cage tightly. "You know nothing of honour and sacrifice. You do not understand what it takes to be a real woman… a woman of Boska."

Abildan seemed surprised. "Excuse me?"

"Had you offered me your tricks at the very beginning, I would have accepted. Had you told me that sacrificing my life to save yours would in turn save Elander, I would have grasped the chance with both hands. Unquestioningly."

Abildan shook her head, bemused. "Stupidity is not as virtuous as you might believe, Sir Vladisal."

"May your remaining days be cursed, feliwyrd."

"Yes, I think they will be."

The Ulyyn warrior on the hawk's back gave a loud click and dug in his heels. The giant bird spread its huge wings and leapt into the air, snatching the cage from the ground after it. Vladisal was jostled inside.

The ground fell away. Abildan raised a hand.

"Luck or fate, Sir Knight?" she called. "Only the Wyrd know for sure. Farewell."

About the Author

Edward Cox is the author of *The Song of the Sycamore*, *The Bone Shaker*, and The Relic Guild Trilogy (*The Relic Guild*, *The Cathedral of Known Things*, *The Watcher of Dead Time*). He lectures in creative writing, has been known to write reviews, and has published a host of short stories over the years, including stories in the Newcon Press anthologies Legends II and Ten Tale Tales. He currently lives in the south east of England where he makes stuff up in his spider-infested garage on a desk that might have once been a functioning tumble dryer.

More New Titles from NewCon Press

David Gullen – Shopocalypse

A Bonnie and Clyde for the Trump era, Josie and Novik embark on the ultimate roadtrip. In a near-future re-sculpted politically and geographically by climate change, they blaze a trail across the shopping malls of America in a printed intelligent car (stolen by accident), with a hundred and ninety million LSD-contaminated dollars in the trunk, buying shoes and cameras to change the world.

Kim Lakin-Smith – Rise

Charged with crimes against the state, Kali Titian (pilot, soldier, and engineer), is sentenced to Erbärmlich prison camp, where few survive for long. Here she encounters Mohab, the Speaker's son, and uncovers two ancient energy sources, which may just bring redemption to an oppressed people. The author of *Cyber Circus* returns with a dazzling tale of courage against the odds and the power of hope.

Andrew Wallace – Celebrity Werewolf

Suave, sophisticated, erudite and charming, Gig Danvers seems too good to be true. Appearing from nowhere, he champions humanitarian causes and revolutionises science,developing the first organic computer to exceed silicon capacity; but are his critics right to be cautious? Is there a darker side to this enigmatic benefactor, one that is more in keeping with his status as the Cleberity Werewolf?

Legends 3 – edited by Ian Whates

David Gemmell passed away in 2006, leaving behind a legacy of memorable characters, and thrilling tales. The *Legends* series of anthologies, of which this the third and almost certainly final volume, is intended to pay homage to one of fantasy fiction's greatest writers. Features a selection of dazzling stories written especially for the books by some of the finest fantasy authors around.

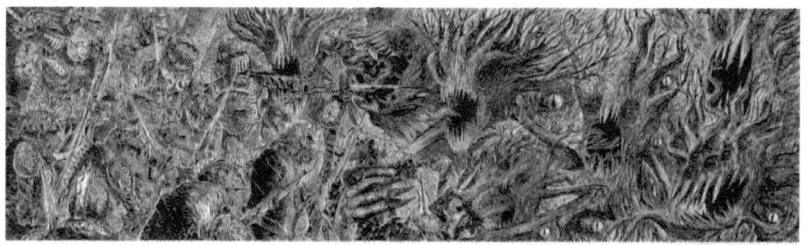

NewCon Press Novella Set 6: Blood and Blade

Four stand-alone novellas of sword play, sorcery, blood-drenched battles, noble deeds and fool-hardy endeavours, linked only by their shared cover art. Released summer 2019, in paperback, limited edition hardback, and as a slipcased set featuring all four novellas as signed hardbacks and **Duncan Kay**'s combined artwork as a wrap-around.

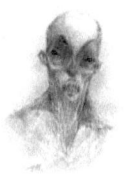

In **Edward Cox**'s *The Bone Shaker,* Sir Vladisal and her knights are lost within endless woodlands. Harried by demons, they seek the kidnapped son of their Duchess, facing terror at every turn. **Gaie Sebold** takes us on *A Hazardous Engagement,* wherein a wily gang of thieves are set an impossible task. Fortunately, they never know when to quit. In *Serpent Rose,* **Kari Sperring** takes us to the realm of Avalon and the intrigues surrounding some of the lesser known knights and characters of King Arthur's court, while in **Gavin Smith**'s *Chivalry* we follow a young

knight from the tourney fields to the battlefield, where he is forced to grow up rapidly as he faces challenges beyond his wildest imaginings.

Four stunning tales of epic fantasy scaled down to novella size by four outstanding authors.

Immanion Press
Purveyors of Speculative Fiction

Strindberg's Ghost Sonata & Other Uncollected Tales by Tanith Lee

This book is the first of three anthologies to be published by Immanion Press that will showcase some of Tanith Lee's most sought-after tales. Spanning the genres of horror and fantasy, upon vivid and mysterious worlds, the book includes a story that has never been published before – 'Iron City' – as well as two tales set in the Flat Earth mythos; 'The Pain of Glass' and 'The Origin of Snow', the latter of which only ever appeared briefly on the author's web site. This collection presents a jewel casket of twenty stories, and even to the most avid fan of Tanith Lee will contain gems they've not read before. ISBN 978-1-912815-00-5, £12.99, $18.99 pbk

A Raven Bound with Lilies by Storm Constantine

The Wraeththu have captivated readers for three decades. This anthology of 15 tales collects all the published Wraeththu short stories into one volume, and also includes extra material, including the author's first explorations of the androgynous race. The tales range from the 'creation story' *Paragenesis*, through the bloody, brutal rise of the earliest tribes, and on into a future, where strange mutations are starting to emerge from hidden corners of the earth. ISBN: 978-1-907737-80-0 £11.99, $15.50 pbk

The Lord of the Looking Glass by Fiona McGavin

The author has an extraordinary talent for taking genre tropes and turning them around into something completely new, playing deftly with topsy-turvy relationships between supernatural creatures and people of the real world. 'Post Garden Centre Blues' reveals an unusual relationship between taker and taken in a twist of the changeling myth. 'A Tale from the End of the World' takes the reader into her developing mythos of a post-apocalyptic world, which is bizarre, Gothic and steampunk all at once. 'Magpie' features a girl scavenging from the dead on a battlefield, whose callous greed invokes a dire curse. Following in the tradition of exemplary short story writers like Tanith Lee and Liz Williams, Fiona has a vivid style of writing that brings intriguing new visions to fantasy, horror and science fiction. ISBN: 978-1-907737-99-2, £11.99, $17.50 pbk

www.immanion-press.com

www.ingramcontent.com/pod-product-compliance
Lightning Source LLC
Chambersburg PA
CBHW020742130626
46554CB00006B/2113